TAKE ME TO THE
CASTLE
F.C. MALBY

First published in the United States of America in
paperback in 2012

This paperback edition published in 2012

Copyright © F. C. Malby, 2012

The moral right of F.C. Malby to be identified as
the author of this work has been asserted in
accordance with the Copyright, Designs and
Patents Act of 1988.

A CIP catalogue record for this book
is available from the British Library.

ISBN: 978 1 47925 3623

In loving memory of my dear friend Meriel

Nothing in this world is hidden forever. The gold, which has lain for centuries unsuspected in the ground, reveals itself one day on the surface. Sand turns traitor, and betrays the footstep that has passed over it.

Wilkie Collins

rev·o·lu·tion

— noun

1. the overthrow of a government
2. fundamental change
3. act or instance of revolving

Chapter 1

Letovice, February 1993

The air was sharp and the sun had long gone. Home felt far away and her loss cut deep into her thoughts, marring the present with its stifling grip. The snow glistened in the evening light, her fur-lined boots kicked through its layers. Something told her that it wouldn't be long, thoughts from a prison cell would come to light, lives shattered by a system she could not understand.

The broken speaker hung from the post above, fallen from its perfectly placed hook – one of the few remaining signs of the old order. Daily announcements and political propaganda could no longer be heard on the streets below. The broadcasts had always felt familiar but things had changed. The news was still regular but with a different tone. The world beyond would encroach on their safety, muscle in with no invitation. Words of her father echoed in her consciousness – warnings, predictions, judgements, hope.

'Jana,' came a voice through the fog. 'Are you all right?' Miloš walked towards her. His tall figure cast a shadow across her path. He stopped just short of her boots and rested his arm on her shoulder, a forward gesture.

'I'm looking for Babička, grandmother, but I'll walk you home. You look cold. Here, take my hat.'

He placed it over her head and walked alongside her, striding purposefully.

'You're quiet this evening. Tell me.'

'Just thinking, nothing in particular.' She glanced up at him. 'I can't believe I've been here for a few months already. Your family has been kind to let me stay, Miloš, really kind.'

He smiled, 'Well, you've added colour, Jana. I'll give you that. Babička's evenings won't be the same without your stories and I'm not sure who Mother will talk to about all her worries. Kamila never has time to listen, she darts around as if she's on fire.'

Their laughs were muffled by the snowfall. 'I kind of like having you around too, if I'm honest. You add a bit of je ne sais quoi.'

'Mess?'

'No, you know what I mean. It'll be different without you.'

They reached the house and walked up the steps to the front door. The house was dark but welcoming, the light obscured by net curtains. It was full of old oil paintings by Miloš's grandfather – pictures of local scenery and some further afield in parts of Bavaria. She knew enough about oil paint to see that he had used a pallet knife. Thick, dark strokes had left wild trees and fields.

The phone rang as they stood in the hallway. Miloš took off his coat, threw it at the chair by the telephone table, and watched his sister grip the receiver.

'She has been with you for a couple of days already?' said Kamila, tapping her fingernails on the table. 'Shall I come and get her?'

'Who is it?' asked Mrs Martinek, listening in from the kitchen. She raised her voice. 'Have they seen her?'

Kamila rolled her eyes. 'We'll see you in half an hour, Mrs Levitska. Thank you, goodbye.'

She hung up and turned towards her mother, who was wearing an old apron and drying a bowl with a blue cloth. The kind of cloth Jana had seen her mother using, with cross-stitching along each end. It reminded her of childhood days, and lines of cloth hanging up to dry by the kitchen window of their apartment.

'Mrs Levitska has had Babička for two days,' said Kamila.

'When is she coming home?' asked Mrs Martinek. She played with the damp cloth and stood in front of Kamila, shuffling from one foot to the other.

'Soon, I think.' Kamila glanced at Miloš.

'She seems to have taken to wandering the village,' said Mrs Martinek. 'These 'neighbourly' visits are lasting longer and longer. Don't these people realise that we're worrying about her?'

'Well, she's coming home now,' said Kamila. 'Let's not make a fuss. There's no need to worry.'

'I'm sure she's been having a wonderful time,' said Miloš.

'Yes, at the expense of my nerves,' said Mrs Martinek.

'But you know how Babička's walks sometimes go on for days,' said Jana. 'She likes to stop at people's homes for a chat. I hear all her stories in the evenings, she laughs as she recalls them. It makes her happy. Happiness is important at her age, isn't it?' Mrs Martinek started to fold the cloth, half listening.

'I don't know if she forgets to come home or if they just assume she's staying.' Miloš laughed but was stopped short by the steely look from his mother.

'Don't any of you care?' she said. Her voice was shaky. Jana looked at her for a moment.

'Of course, but she'll be fine, you'll see,' said Jana.

Kamila laid the table. She set out six places, lifted the last mat off the lace tablecloth, stood still for a moment, and put it back.

'Kamila, she'll be back in time for a meal, you can put it down.' Jana took the cutlery out of the drawer and placed her hand gently on Kamila's back. The drawer was one of many in a dark wood cabinet behind the dining table. It had shelves higher up with a healthy collection of spirits, and an eclectic mix of glazed pottery and artefacts. A pile of carefully placed lace cloths lay between the shelves and the drawers. The house was full of lace tablecloths, place mats and headrests for

4

armchairs, all made by Babička at one time or another.

'It's not that we don't know everyone in the village,' said Mrs Martinek. Maybe she was trying to reassure herself. 'I'm never quite sure whether she really gets lost or simply loses all sense of time.'

To Jana's mind everybody seemed happy to see Babička and resisted returning her, like a misplaced package sent to the wrong address. It was as if the recipient opened it up, knowing it should be returned, but wondering how long they could legitimately keep it before being charged with theft by the Martinek family.

Jana wandered into the kitchen, picked up the kettle and filled it from the tap that dripped sporadically. Mr Martinek had said that he was going to fix it. He always said he was going to fix it. Her father would have fixed it by now. She started to light the stove to heat the water.

'Jana,' said Kamila, 'are you are wearing my brother's hat?' It sounded incriminating.

'Am I?' She patted her head absent-mindedly. 'You're right, he lent it to me.'

Mrs Martinek put down the cloth, straightened out her apron, and watched the scene from the stool in the corner of the kitchen.

'I bumped into him and he lent it to me. What's the big deal? It's a hat. It's cold outside. Tea, anyone?'

'I'll have a coffee.' Miloš rescued the conversation. 'Don't give me any of that dishwater stuff. What is it, fruit tea? Tastes revolting if you ask me.'

'Well, we're not asking,' Kamila interrupted, 'and I'll have a camomile.' She grabbed the cloth from her mother and swiped Miloš across the back of his legs. It was an action that had been perfectly honed through years of practice. He feigned pain. 'Ouch!'

Chapter 2

Prague, May 1979

The doorbell woke them up. Jana knew that it wasn't yet morning because the darkness hid behind the curtains where it belonged. The shadows from the street lamps left outlines on the wooden chair by the door, much like the figures she had seen on the television once. She looked across the room at Irena and could hear faint breaths from her sister's bed. Trying not to wake her, Jana slid out from under the blankets and opened the bedroom door just enough to view the front door of the apartment in silence.

'Who is it?' Her mother's voice sounded shaky. She could see her father following closely behind – they were wearing dressing gowns – and Jana could just about see her father gesturing something she didn't understand. Her mother's hair was tied in an obligatory night time plait. Her father reached down to secure the second slipper. They looked agitated, as if they were expecting the caller.

There was silence from outside the door of the apartment and her father unlocked it slowly, as though he was trying not to disturb a nest of bees. She had overheard her parents talking about the 'early morning knock at the door', as they called it, and rumours of friends being taken away in the dark, but she thought that they were immune – protected, removed from it. Her father had always told her that the truth would prevail, not that she really knew what he meant. Jana believed that they would be shielded from bad things, from things that would harm them.

The door opened slowly and she could see the outline of five men standing in the corridor. Her room was far enough away from the figures for no one to notice her nose pressing into the door frame. She was aware of her own breathing and tried to slow it down, slow down her heartbeat until she was invisible. The idea in these moments is to be completely invisible. There were a lot of invisible people in Prague, doing invisible things to invisible people. Or so she had heard from friends whose families had encountered the 'knock at the door'.

The teasing at school now seemed silly. She didn't think it was funny – not now, not in that moment. How could she stop the men from taking one of them away? Who had they come for?

'Radek Maček?' one of the figures asked as he stepped into

their apartment.

The look on Matka's face triggered fear in Jana. How did they know her father's name? Shouldn't they be asleep too?

'Yes,' he responded. 'What do you want?'

'You are wanted for questioning.'

Jana caught her breath. She could see that this was not a playground joke or a dream. She was very much awake now. Her brother, Aleš, didn't seem to have stirred from the next room, and she could still hear her sister's slow breathing. She wanted to still be asleep, wanted not to see this. Her parents looked calm from the outside but she knew that something was wrong from the tone of their voices.

The conversation went on and everything looked normal, as though the visitors had been invited. She knew they hadn't, not at this hour. The black leather jackets crinkled and squeaked as they moved into the apartment, surrounding Tatínek and Matka. They looked frightened now. She was frightened.

'It's just routine.'

'The children are asleep. Please.' Matka pleaded with them.

Jana knew that she should have run back to bed, hidden under the sheets. Something stopped her, feet bolted to the floor, heart racing like a rabbit chased by dogs.

'We'll come back.'

'Back? No!' Jana rolled the thoughts through her tired head. They can't come back. I won't let them. 'Tatínek!' She wanted to shout out his name at the top of her voice but she couldn't, not with the shadows in the apartment. She swallowed the word, not to be repeated to his face for some time.

It was difficult to see what was going on, except for the light coming through the kitchen window. It rested on a section of the cold floor in the hallway, a long way from its source. The jackets moved around a bit. Then they took Tatínek and led him towards the door. One lingered by the bookcase.

'What's this?' he demanded, pulling out volumes of Tatínek's work. There was a gap, long enough for her to count at least three breaths.

'Just some economics papers, nothing interesting.'

'Well, *we'll* decide what's interesting,' said the shadow.

His voice sounded teasing and menacing all at the same time. Why were they looking at Tatínek's books? Did they want to read one? Jana could feel the blood running cold in her veins. She couldn't feel her toes, and the night air made her shiver. *They* made her shiver.

The shadows left with her dear Tatínek. The door closed firmly behind them. Why did he go? He could have said no to them. He could have stopped them. Deep down something told her that he couldn't have stopped them, even if he had tried.

Matka dropped to her knees, clasping her head in her hands somewhere deep in her lap. She sobbed silently. The light caught the back of her plait. It looked pretty. The confusion frightened Jana. She wanted to run to Matka to reassure her, but she couldn't, not with fear in her eyes.

Jana moved quietly back to bed and slipped under the

covers. She grabbed the rag doll, well worn and comforting. Everything was normal, everything was all right, just as it was before the shadows came that night. Her heart betrayed her, threatening to jump out of the covers. She tried again – deep breathing to slow it down, slow down her heartbeat, her breath.

The next morning was the same as any other, except for the absence of Tatínek. Matka mentioned something about him going to work early. Jana chose to ignore it. Irena and Aleš played with bits of ham and cheese. Jana pushed some bread around her plate. She felt too sick to eat. Matka poured herself some coffee.

'Jana, is everything all right, my love? You seem quiet.'

'Yes, Maminka, I'm fine. I'm just not that hungry.'

'Are you sick? You look pale.' She reached across the table to feel Jana's forehead.

'No, it's OK. I'm OK.' Jana longed to ask her mother if she was fine, if Tatínek was fine. Where did they take him? Who were the men? There were so many questions that she could not ask. It would be like opening a basket of snakes and not being able get them back in again. They might hiss or bite.

Aleš waved a piece of cheese in the air. 'She's dreaming,' he said, 'dreaming of a day without school, dreaming of holidays in the mountains, aren't you?'

'Yes, something like that,' Jana smiled, as if to thank him for rescuing her. Irena started to clear the plates when there was a knock at the door. Matka froze. Jana caught her breath. Was this the coming back that they talked about? The

11

shadows? The jackets?

Aleš and Irena carried on with the morning routine, oblivious to their fear. Irena stacked plates by the sink and Aleš scrabbled around for his bag and shoes like a dog looking for a bone. His hair was a mess, it was always a mess. He never seemed to care. Jana spent ages brushing her long tawny hair each morning. Its thickness made the job all the more difficult. She gazed into the mirror at her green eyes and wondered who she most resembled, if at all.

Matka opened the door slowly. It was the same scene as last night, only without the dressing gown, the plait and, of course, Tatínek.

Her brother and sister had happily accepted the story that he was at work, and why shouldn't they? Why would they believe what Jana had seen in the early hours of the morning – the questions, the disappearance of their father? The daylight made it less sinister, but she was still afraid.

'Mrs Maček?' one of them asked.

'Yes.' She hesitated. 'What can I do for you?'

There were only three shadows now. Matka behaved as though their call was perfectly normal, that nothing was wrong, that Tatínek really was at work.

'We have orders to search the premises.'

She stepped away from the door and let them past. The jackets marched in and scanned the bookshelves and the doors leading from the hallway. They headed towards Tatínek's study like an army heading for combat.

'Who are they?' Irena uttered the question that had been on

Jana's mind since their first visit.

'Just some officers, they need to look for something.' Matka used her voice that said 'Don't ask me any more questions'. The one she used when they were in the car asking when they would get home. This time she sounded cold, afraid even.

'What do they want?' Irena persisted.

'Just some papers of your father's. It's OK.'

Jana ran to the study door and watched. The men were undisturbed by their audience.

'Ah, found them,' Aleš announced, waving something in the air.

'What's that?' Matka asked, not really needing the answer. She followed the men into the study and watched them pull papers and books out of the over-packed shelves.

'My shoes, I've found them.' No one much cared about the shoes.

The jackets scanned the room and lifted up the typewriter, the one that her father used almost daily. It had become part of the study furniture, it almost became part of Tatínek, too, when he wrote. He spent hours typing with those dark sheets in between bits of paper that made copies of things, of words – words that the men seemed to be looking for.

'What's this?' One of them waved a letter in the air accusingly. He held up some of the papers from the pile, now strewn across the table.

The others moved in like a wake of vultures, ready to devour their prey. She had seen it on television once.

'Scavengers,' Tatínek called them. They swoop in and feed off the carcasses of animals that are too weak to escape – lots of them on battlefields. This looked the same, only the victim wasn't there, just his writing, his typewriter, and bits of dark paper.

Jana hung on to the doorframe. Her mother knew she was there – this time they were all awake. Watching last night, when he could defend himself, had been frightening. It was worse now seeing them rummage through his study, and his things, while he was not there.

One of the others started reading something. 'Vaclav Havel Memorandum. Charter 77. What's this?' He took another paper. 'Committee for the Defense of the Unjustly Prosecuted, April 1979.'

'Enemy of the State!' One of them shouted. 'Seize the typewriter. Take the carbon copies as well, the books, the papers, all of it. We need all the evidence.'

'Traitor,' they conferred.

What's a traitor? Was it a bad thing? She wondered.

They stormed out with a look of satisfaction and disgust. How could Tatínek have done something bad? He was a good man, a good father. He always did what was right. Where was he? The shadows marched out with their 'traitor' things, Tatínek's things. Matka pushed the door, dropping her head against it as it closed.

Chapter 3

Prague, October 1992

The notebooks that Lukas held in his hands were worn and thin, smaller than he remembered. The words contained in the spiral-bound pages could incriminate, inform, accuse, trap, frame, bear witness to many lives. You could choose any of these words and the result would be almost the same. Almost, but not quite – one word was the method by which the state collected their information. They could reel in the informants and spread them out like tentacles, ready to sting in any direction, poisoning the victims with venom. Complicit with the system, they would do their job in silence, inform. The memories haunted him in the small hours.

The names on the crumpled sheets of paper provided a mine of information, information that would give them power.

He leafed through the pages reluctantly, his hand shaking slightly. The informant had been ordered to feed these pages to the secret police. He needed reminding that it was the work of a person no longer under state control. There had been no choice. The system was so penetrating that living with those decisions was hard to bear. The end of the regime was a yesterday. Before that it was always a tomorrow, a future or a never.

The phone rang.

Lukas slipped the notebooks in between the collection of books by Havel on the shelf. No one would see them or find them. He needed to keep them. For whatever reason, he needed to keep them.

'Benes, great to hear you. Congratulations. When's the big day? Are you free this evening? We should celebrate with a few beers.'

He fiddled with his pen and started to draw on the small piece of paper by the phone. 'Great, let's talk then. See you around seven, usual place.'

Today approached without warning. Already late for the meeting, he grabbed his well-worn brown jacket and ran down the stone staircase and on to the street. Just catching the number twenty-two tram to Pražský Hrad, he found a seat by an open window. Breathing in the city air, Lukas watched the Skodas and people passing – mothers with small children, men in suits, buskers, students. It looked like a scene from a Kokoschka painting, a frenetic picture, refusing to stand still.

The tram wound its way through the streets, stopping

briefly at traffic lights. The familiar bell sounded as a warning to people and cars crossing the tracks as it approached. He had never actually seen anyone crash into one of these heavy contraptions, but he could recall a few near misses.

The meeting had already started when he entered the room in the castle offices on Hradčany Hill. The walls were white with little detail, except for the obligatory painting of the president. An expressionless official – the chair of the meeting, he assumed – stood up and welcomed him.

'This is Lukas Dobransky, one of our top conservators. Lukas, meet the men from the Getty Conservation Institute. I presume that you already know the officials from the Office of the President, and the Castle Administration Team.'

The chair ran through the names and took a seat at the top of the rectangular arrangement of tables. There was hand shaking and nodding. Lukas sat down quickly, hoping that the introductions had not been repeated for his benefit.

'So, without delay,' began the expressionless chair, 'The Last Judgement mosaic of the Cathedral of St. Vitus. The conservation project is high on the president's agenda. We need to look at ways in which we can clean and treat the mosaic in order to slow down the erosion.' He ran his hand through his hair and continued.

'We have drafted in these two gentlemen who worked on the Vitale Church in Ravenna, Italy. I think you're all familiar with their work, and I would like to thank them for agreeing to share their expertise with us.'

One of the Italians was large with a dark beard and round

17

glasses, older. The younger of the two wore a tweed jacket and clutched several notebooks. He looked keen and nervous. Lukas had seen this type of newcomer before, like a puppy, eager to please its master. The chair reached for his coffee and nodded to a second official who continued almost immediately.

'Thank you to you all for agreeing to work with us on this project. As you know, it is one of the finest pieces of monumental, medieval mosaic art in Europe.' A few heads nodded. 'We are proud to call it a piece of the fabric of our history. What is needed here is for us to carefully decide on the method of intervention.'

The official laid out the options. 'We can remove the mosaic and house it in a less erosive environment, replacing it with a copy.'

The tweeded Italian grimaced and looked at his bearded partner. Lukas looked down at his pen, took a gulp of water and forced himself not to fiddle. He winced at the thought of removing the tiles. It would never work.

The official continued. 'Or we can simply treat it in its current location.' Lukas felt a wave of relief.

The conservator to Lukas's left started tapping his right foot. He responded first. 'The damage to an already eroded mosaic would become too great if we were to remove it. Are you sure it is even a feasible option?' He was met with brief glances from across the room.

'But housing it somewhere safer would prevent further erosion,' said the official, 'or indeed the need for further treatment in the next twenty to thirty years. Mr Ricceri, perhaps you could share with us your experience with the Vitale mosaics.' He waited for a response from the Italian.

'Certainly,' replied the bearded man. 'We began with a pilot project to determine the appropriate method of conservation for the tesserae. It was decided not to remove the pieces but to work *in situ.*'

'We wanted minimal interference,' the tweed added. 'We began with an acrylic resin coating and the cracked tiles were cleaned with ammonium bicarbonate.'

'Yes, thank you,' said an imposing Getty spokesman, sitting next to the chair of the meeting. 'Your work has been well recognised. Your tiles are glass, as are ours. It will be important to look at the causes of deterioration and consider the options for treatment *in situ*, if this is the route we decide to take.'

'Lukas? Any thoughts?' the chair asked. Lukas's eyes had been focused on the picture of Vaclav Havel on the wall above the window. 'A fine man,' said the chair, glancing in the direction of the painting.

Lukas coughed and took another sip of water. 'Yes, I would agree with Mr Ricceri. I think the removal of the mosaic is too high a risk, and the potential for further damage is considerable. I would recommend that we try a protective coating for the glass surface of the tiles. We would need to experiment in order to produce the correct coating.' He rubbed his top lip, and rotated his pencil, spinning it on its axis.

'It would take some time, said Lukas, 'but I think this

might be a way forward. I'm sure our Italian friends can help us with their expertise.' Lukas held the palm of his hand out in the direction of the tweed and the beard.

'But a successful solution has not yet been found,' voiced another official. 'They tried during previous restorations here at the castle. This is not the Sistine Chapel fresco and, even if it were, I would be surprised if Michelangelo or the Vatican would approve of a fancy coating.' There were a few smirks from across the room.

The bearded Italian responded carefully. 'Well, they managed to restore it as early as the fifteenth century but I agree it did not last for long.'

'Yes,' said the Getty spokesman, 'but we need a more scientific approach.' He looked squarely at Lukas, who looked up from his scribblings.

'Advances in research make it possible to conceive of a treatment with longer-lasting effects,' said Lukas. 'The tesserae need to be analysed for the types of damage, the areas covered and for evidence of previous treatments.'

'Technology must assist and not interfere with the process of conserving the mosaic,' added a second member of the Getty team. 'Thank you for your contribution, Mr. Dobransky. Any thoughts from the scientific advisors?'

'Well,' said the figure opposite Lukas, 'the grey dust, formed by the corrosion, has been sitting comfortably on the tesserae for many years, and considerable skill will be needed to remove it. The rainwater has reacted with the impurities – the potassium and calcium – within the glass. Water causes the

20

minerals to leach out. The alkaline salts react with the carbon dioxide and sulphur dioxide to form crystals.'

The chair turned to the photographs of the complete mosaic on a board behind him. 'What if we overlay the larger image with smaller transparency sheets to take a closer look at the tesserae? We can then obtain a piece-by-piece record of what is missing, what has been eroded, and assess the damage on a smaller scale.'

There were murmurs of approval around the table.

Words like 'record' and 'damage' made him shudder. Nothing could stop his mind from being catapulted back to the past in one sharp second. Keeping his hands busy, fiddling with something, anything, kept him here in the present.

As the meeting drew to a close Lukas looked at his watch. It had gone on for longer than expected and he needed to get moving. He shook hands with the Italians, and several other members of the team, and slipped out of the room. He had developed a crushing headache during the meeting that felt like a vice around his skull. His face was tight, and he could feel the tension running into his neck and shoulders.

Finding his way back out of the building he threw his arms in the air and swung them in circles above his head. The cobbles dropped away from underneath his feet as he walked downhill and he scanned the city skyline. It was early days in a very long project but there was always something uniquely satisfying about achieving the unachievable.

Lukas pulled his sweater off and threw it over one shoulder. The view over the hanging gardens and rooftops was intoxicating.

As he reached the bar, he could see Benes through the window. He swung the door open and went inside. His friend was at the usual table in the corner of the bar by the window with two glasses of beer.

'Thanks, good to see you.' He shook Benes' hand and sat down on the wooden stool opposite.

'Sorry I'm late. The meeting ran on longer than expected. I should be buying you a beer.'

'It's not a problem. I got here early. So, how's the elusive Lukas?'

'Meaning?'

'I haven't been able to reach you on the phone until today.'

'Sorry, too much to get done. I've been in and out of various meetings. I won't bore you with the details. We aren't here to talk about me. Here's to the courageous man. Na zdravi.'

Lukas raised his beer and clinked glasses with his friend. 'Congratulations, Benes. When did it all happen?'

Benes swirled the beer around his glass. He looked up with a sparkle in his eye. 'At the weekend, I took Irena to the ballet. She's a big fan. Then, as we crossed the bridge on the way home, I got down on one knee. I wanted to do it properly.'

'Impressive. And she said yes?'

'Yes, although the pause was long enough to make me break out into a sweat. I've been waiting for the right time. I'm not sure that there is a right time but I want to be with her.'

'So that's why you've been looking happy lately.' Lukas

smiled.

'Have I?' Benes raised his eyebrows, and took a sip of beer.

'Yes, you've been different over the past few weeks, months, I don't know how long.'

'I've wanted to ask her for a long time. Do you think you'll get married?'

Lukas glanced out of the window. 'I don't know, Benes. I'm not sure I've ever really understood women enough for that kind of commitment.' He flipped his beer mat up in the air with his index finger and caught it in his hand. 'I'm too busy for a relationship right now.'

Lukas felt his chest tighten. These kinds of questions made him uncomfortable. Work provided a safe haven where he didn't have to think about his life and his relationships, or lack of them. It was a place where he was respected, where he was good at something. Most of his colleagues knew little about him outside the meetings and workshops. He liked it that way.

Benes broke the silence. 'Don't get so busy that you squeeze it all out – time for people. It's not as scary as you think.'

'I'm not. I'm good. Like I said, it's just not a good time for me at the moment.'

'When was the last time you saw a girl, or any other friend?'

Benes wasn't going to relent in a hurry. Lukas hated these kinds of questions. He lit a cigarette and inhaled deeply. He exhaled slowly.

'I don't know, why does it matter? To you, I mean?'

'It matters to me because you look sad, troubled. I'm not sure. I'm just worried about you and I don't like the thought of you being…'

'Single?' Lukas finished the sentence.

Benes sat back and kicked his feet out. 'I'm here, but I can't meet you every week. Not to start with.'

Lukas frowned and studied his friend. 'I don't need you. I don't need people. I'm alright as I am. I'm happy with my work and I don't need a girlfriend, or a wife, for that matter. No offence.'

'None taken.'

It was easy to compartmentalise things – work was work, and home was home. The last girl had gone on and on about something to do with him not expressing his feelings, and being defensive and guarded. It left him feeling worse about himself. He reached across the table and picked up Benes' empty glass.

'Let me get you another.'

'Great.' Lukas disappeared to the bar, where the young girl smiled and placed two full glasses down on the counter. She leaned forward and looked at him for long enough to make him feel ill-at-ease. He picked them up without saying a word, and walked back to the table by the window.

'I think she likes you.'

'Who?'

'The girl at the bar, the one with the low top that you pretended not to notice.'

'Don't be ridiculous. We're different, Benes. We need

different things. You want to settle down. I want to restore things, travel, stay in with a beer and read, go out when I feel like it.'

'Marriage isn't a life sentence. Although you do a good job of making it sound like one.'

'Don't use that word.'

'What? Marriage?'

'No. Sentence. You don't know what it means.'

Benes pulled away from the table. Lukas could see that the conversation was getting too intense, and he backed down. He valued his friend's wisdom but he was afraid. Moments like these made his heart race and the palms of his hands moist. He despised so many of his past actions but this was normal life and he was supposed to react like a normal person.

'Thanks for the beer,' said Benes. 'So what was the meeting about? New project?'

Relieved by the change of subject, Lukas could feel his shoulders and face muscles begin to relax.

'We're trying to find a way of restoring a castle mosaic. It's the main mosaic over the Golden Gate. It will be beautiful if we can clean it properly.'

'I'm not sure that I've seen it.' Benes put his hands behind his head. He breathed out slowly.

'I would imagine most people miss it. The tiles are so heavily eroded and covered in dirt that it will take years of work. If we can get through all of the grey you will be able to see around thirty-one shades of coloured glass.'

'That's impressive. How many tiles are we talking about?'

Few people ever asked about the details.

'Somewhere around a million. It's eighty-four square metres, so it's going to be a huge task.'

'Well, they've picked the right man for the job. You're not short of experience.'

'Thanks. I just need to read a lot more material before the next meeting. The Getty Institute specialists are reviewing the scientific documents and I need to look at them myself so that I'm up to date. The team is interesting. It's a huge project that will involve years and years of research and restoration.'

'It's good to see you enjoying your work, Lukas. Don't look now, but she's coming over.'

'Who?'

'Your friend at the bar, she's nice.'

'Benes don't do this.'

Lukas felt a hand on his shoulder and dropped his glass. It shattered into jagged pieces in a pool of honey-coloured liquid by his feet.

'I'm sorry,' she said, 'I didn't mean to startle you.'

'It's OK. I was just leaving.'

Lukas jumped up and shook his friend's hand.

'Are you alright?' said Benes, looking puzzled.

'Yes. Got to go. I'll call you.' He left swiftly.

Turning left to walk back up the hill, he looked in through the window. Lukas could see his friend and the girl clearing the mess. They were having an intense conversation. His stomach sank in a familiar way that made him feel utterly powerless.

Chapter 4

Letovice, March 1993

Jana watched Miloš as he picked up the book and started leafing through it on the sofa. His steely blue eyes scanned the pages and his hands hovered over the words like a magician.

'Physiology,' she said, hoping he might respond.

'Yes, I'm just looking. Lots to learn before I start medicine.' He looked up at her and smiled. 'What?'

'Nothing,' I was just trying to imagine you as a doctor, a surgeon, maybe.

'Thought about surgery. No, Paediatrics is more along the lines of what I want to do.'

'Children? Babies?' she waited.

He looked up at her, this time for longer. 'And what is wrong with that?'

She giggled, 'Just can't picture you with babies. I thought you wanted to do tropical medicine.'

'Well you live and learn, don't you? Why does it seem so strange to you?'

'I don't know, you seem too … just too…I imagine paediatricians to be gentle, maternal, paternal, whatever it is that makes them just right with children.'

'Well, Jana, the world is not always as it seems through your eyes.'

'Really? And what might the world through my eyes look like, Doctor Martinek?'

'I'm not a doctor … yet. I was just saying.'

'Yes?'

'I was just saying that you don't have to pigeon hole people or second guess everyone.' He watched the look of surprise on her face. 'Jana, I just think you need to relax, be a bit more open minded in your opinions, that's all.'

'Miloš, just because you read, just because you have plays and books on Czech literature, it doesn't make you a genius. It doesn't make you a better person.'

'No, I just like to read. I like to learn.'

He had talked about lots of things that he learned, things that she found fascinating. He was less fascinating now and more opinionated. He said he wanted to travel, at least beyond Hungary, and see the world. Who didn't? Well, she didn't. Her corner of the world was alright as it was. She stood up and left the room.

Mr Martinek walked into the room with his pipe and a

paper. 'What's going on? Are we going to eat? I'm hungry.'

'You're always hungry, miláčku darling. Mrs Levitska should be here soon with Babička, with any luck,' said Mrs Martinek. 'She's been off again on one of her adventures, to the detriment of my frail nerves.'

Jana brought the food through into the front room and laid it on the lace tablecloth. They all took their seats, each sitting in their usual places. Jana had assumed a seat next to Kamila, making her feel like a permanent fixture. She had a view of Miloš from across the table, although tonight she avoided his gaze.

They passed meatballs and bread around the table. There was a knock at the door. Mrs Levitska proceeded to let herself in and presented Babička to them like a trophy.

'I'm sorry not to have let you know sooner. She's fine, no need to worry. Something smells lovely. I haven't been harbouring a criminal, just your mother. She's back now.'

'Not to worry, didn't notice she'd gone,' said Mr Martinek. 'Just in time for food. Would you like to join us?'

Mrs Martinek looked up at him swiftly.

'Come on, Babička,' said Miloš. 'Come and join us. I'll get you a plate.' He jumped out of his seat. Jana watched him as he disappeared into the kitchen. Mrs Levitska saw the look on Mrs Martinek's face and slipped away quietly, closing the door behind her.

After dinner Miloš pulled out a travel book from the pile that he had squirreled away, as though the winter had created a shortage of material. He and his father poured out some beers and Kamila stood in the kitchen, calming her mother's nerves.

Jana was happy to escape and took Babička upstairs to her room, holding her arm on the stairs. Sometimes she would read to her and sometimes Babička sang to Jana. This evening, she sat on her rocking chair in the corner of the room. Looking at the picture of her wedding day on the wall, she began to sing.

'*Jak se máš, jak se máš?*
How are you?
How's your father, mother, sister
and your brother?
Jak se máš, jak se máš?'

She tapped her foot in time with the notes, and strummed her fingers on the curved wooden arm of the rocking chair as it rolled back and forth. She had a faraway look in her eyes.

'It's a friendly greeting when you meet another.
Hey there, Joe, don't you know.
It's a grand ole way to say Hello, how are you?'

Jana clapped. 'Does Mrs Martinek know where you've been when you go out, Babička?'

'No, dear. No need to bother them with my whereabouts.' She stopped for a moment. 'Don't you think it's a beautiful evening? Clearest skies I've seen in a long time.'

Jana sighed. 'Lovely. You know that they worry. We all worry a little when you go out and don't come back.'

'I remember when Franek asked me to marry him. I was your age, nineteen.' Babička's face was full of excitement. 'He was a handsome thing and I knew when he pulled out a ring.'

She held out her left hand for Jana to admire her engagement ring, which now looked loose on her frail finger. The small sapphires sat either side of a neat diamond. It had withstood the decades of marriage, family and life, and the band now looked thin and fragile. Her face, though, looked fresh and childlike as she spoke. Her eyes sparkled as they might have done on that night.

The lines in the corners of her eyes spoke of years of wisdom, as a tree with the number of rings increasing with each passing year. She was a small frame of a woman with piercing eyes that suggested that they knew you, understood you even. Eyes that had seen good and bad, eyes that had smiled, eyes that had endured hardship, eyes that had enjoyed life and family. She almost sang as she spoke. The notes in her voice varied according to what she said. In her excitement it would rise to a crescendo.

'I remember thinking, this is it, this is the man that I'm going to marry. So many years of happiness and now I have my wonderful grandchildren to show for it. You know Miloš is a handsome boy.'

She looked at Jana for a moment with an unwavering gaze, and then played with her ring.

'Girls like him. He will make a good husband and a good father one day. He's older than Kamila, so he'll inherit my house. I haven't been able to live in it on my own for some years now.'

Jana nodded, understanding the message. She acknowledged the sentiments and took Babička's hand, holding it gently. Her skin was soft and transparent.

'I'm so proud of them,' said Babička. She rested her other hand on top of Jana's. 'As I was of him. He loved me, and worked hard for us all. He was always so kind and thoughtful, such fun. I knew then that he would make me happy, and I really believed I could do the same. We were happy.' Her voice faded as she reminisced. 'I miss him, you know. He was so fond of them all, and he loved big family mealtimes.'

'I know, Babička. I know you miss him.'

Jana was aware that the family did not always have the time to listen to Babička's stories. Many were repeated from time to time. This one, though, she thought was a gem. She untied the scarf from Babička's head, swept the strands of hair back behind her ears and unpinned her bun. Her hair was long and thick, and fell down between her shoulder blades. Jana wrapped a knitted shawl around Babička, reached for the enamelled brush on the dressing table, and ran it through the silver strands. She leaned down and kissed her on the forehead. Her skin smelt of a sweet combination of baking and perfume.

'Good night, Babička, see you tomorrow.'

Jana laid her nightdress out on the bed and left the room with the door slightly open. Mrs Martinek always checked on her mother just before she went to bed.

Babička was up early. Mrs Martinek was trying to stop her

from leaving the house again, without making her feel that she was under house arrest. Miloš followed Jana into the kitchen after breakfast.

'I'm going down to the shop to pick up some groceries for Mother. I want to see what's on at the cinema over the weekend. Will you join me?'

Jana tried not to look surprised. 'I'm not sure, Miloš. I have to get some paperwork ready for tomorrow.'

He took her arm. 'Jana, I'm sorry if I upset you yesterday. I just say things as they are. I thought you would be ok with it but I over-stepped the mark.'

'The papers can wait, give me a minute.' She piled the plates on to the sideboard and went upstairs to apply a fresh coat of lipstick, re-emerging with the scarf that Babička had knitted for her.

'Are you going for a walk? Can I join you?' said Kamila.

'Sure, let's go.' Miloš looked ruffled and began to pace across the floor, while Kamila fumbled around in the cupboard for her coat.

'Kamila?' said Mrs Martinek. 'It's Gabi on the phone. She wants to chat to you about next week.'

'You both go ahead,' said Kamila, looking at Jana. 'I'll catch you later. It's too cold for me.'

Jana caught the look of relief on Miloš's face. He opened the door and she thanked him, stepping out into the snow and down the steps. It was beginning to melt and glisten in the sunlight. She picked up a ball of snow and waited until he had closed the door behind them. As he turned around she hurled it at his head. It almost missed but just about reached its target.

'Got you.'

Miloš opened his mouth and bent down to pick up some ammunition from the heap of snow at the bottom of the steps. Before he had stood up, Jana raced off in the direction of the village. She could hear his footsteps getting closer, but she was running out of steam and collapsed in a heap just by the shop. The sensation of cold ice being rammed down the inside of her jacket was intense. Melting, as it made contact with her skin, she felt the cold shock run down her spine and let out a scream. Miloš stood over her with a look of satisfaction.

Jana glanced up at him with her teeth clenched, suddenly realising she was at his mercy. He was clearly faster and stronger and, although she could outwit him most of the time, he had won today's battle. It made her feel strangely close to him. They were finally alone. He smiled and offered her his scarf to wipe her neck. She refused, but took his hand and he pulled her up out of the snow.

As they looked at her imprint in the snow he suddenly threw himself down into the powder, making a larger hole in the white covering, and was completely motionless.

'Come on, let's go.' Miloš jumped up and took her hand. 'We need bread, milk and some other things.'

'Potatoes, butter, flour – your mother wants to make dumplings.'

'We've picked the wrong day. There's never much here by Friday.'

He led her around the small village shop and paid for the

items. Any vegetables, other than potatoes, were an expensive luxury. Miloš pulled a few korunas out of his pocket and handed over the coins. They loaded up the bag that she had remembered to bring and stepped out into the snow.

They walked towards the cinema, both searching for words to say. Jana was the first to break the silence.

'I really want to see the new film, *The Bodyguard*. I think it starts this weekend.'

He watched her pull her hair back and reposition her hat.

'I read about that,' he said. 'Witney Houston, isn't it? Bit girly, but I think I could manage it.' Miloš smiled and looked at his feet.

'It's got subtitles but your English is good, isn't it?'

'It's OK. Russian or German would be easier, but I like the films coming over from the States.'

'There are a lot of plays on your bookshelves. Do you like theatre?'

'Yes, but I really enjoy films now that we can see decent cinema. Are you warm enough?' He started to put his arm around her, but she could feel his hesitation.

'Yes, fine – I'm always fine.'

'I know. You're a curious one. I can't figure you out.'

'What do you mean?' Jana felt a little insulted by his remark.

'You don't really seem to need much. You're quite, I don't know, self-sufficient.'

'That's good, isn't it?' She wasn't sure what he was implying.

'I can't help wondering what you're hiding. I hope that doesn't upset you.'

'Nothing, Miloš. Nothing, I'm just me. I'm just what you see.' Jana folded her arms and stepped up her pace.

'The screen in Letovice is quite small,' he said quickly, his pace catching up with hers. 'The cinemas in the city are probably bigger.'

'I don't know. I haven't been to this one yet.' She glanced back at him. 'Haven't you been to Prague?'

'No. I'd like to go some time. It looks so beautiful from what I've seen.'

'It is. It's indefinable. So much atmosphere, so many memories.' She was surprised that he talked about the city as if it were alien to him. Jana felt his hand brush past hers as they walked side by side. Her heart quickened and her cheeks flushed. She tried not to respond, in case it had been unintentional. She liked his appearance. He looked young for his age. His eyes showed kindness, curiosity. He was gentle, particularly with his frail grandmother.

'I like spending time with you, Jana. You make me smile.'

She looked at him for a moment, and turned away. 'Do I?'

'Yes, you do. You see things differently. You see people the way they really are. You talk to Babička as if she's the most important person in the world.'

'She's an amazing woman, Miloš. She has so much to share, so much to say. She's interesting and I care about her.'

'I know. I feel bad that we don't give her the time that she needs. Everyone is always too busy and Father just speaks in words of no more than one syllable.'

'Yes, he's a bit short with her but she isn't his mother and you're all living in the same house. We're all living in the same house.'

'Strange, isn't it? Isn't it odd for you? I mean, us being in the same house?'

'I don't know. It wasn't at first but it is a bit now. I try not to talk to you too much in front of them.' The sound of the word 'us' echoed in her head like a new word in a different language.

Miloš smiled. 'I've been thinking about applying to go to the Philippines. They need help with basic medical care in Davao.' She watched him as he continued. 'It's in the south of the country and there are lots of organisations doing voluntary work, lots of opportunities. I wouldn't get paid, but it would be a good start before studying medicine. What do you think?'

'It's what you want, isn't it?' she said. 'It sounds like a good opportunity and I think you've already made up your mind. Why are you asking me what I think?'

Jana fiddled with the buckle on the belt of her jacket and kept her eyes fixed on where her feet were going.

'How long?'

'Just for the summer. You'll be away for your sister's wedding.'

'Right, yes.' She bit her bottom lip.

'Jana, stop.' He turned her towards him, and put his hand on her cheek.

'What's bothering you?'

Miloš lifted her chin and pulled her into his chest. She could feel her eyes welling up, but she fought back the tears. They weren't tears for him. She hoped he wouldn't see. She needed it to stop. The pain caught her at unexpected moments. Sometimes there was a trigger, and sometimes it was completely unprovoked, but it was always there, like a grizzly bear lurking behind a tree. It would catch her unawares and grip her tightly, refusing to let go.

'I'm alright. Just tired, I think.'

'Shall we head home? I'll take you to the cinema tomorrow night.'

'Great.' She blinked hard and pulled her wool hat down over her forehead.

As they reached the front door, Babička waved from her bedroom window.

'Where have you been?' Kamila sounded exasperated.

'The shop,' said Miloš. 'Remember? You were going to join us until your friend called.'

'Gabi, yes.' Kamila looked across at Jana. 'Are you all right?'

'Yes, fine. We got the shopping.'

'OK. Come on in. Don't leave the door open. Lunch is ready.' Kamila walked through to the kitchen, followed by the others.

'We've only just had breakfast,' said Miloš, patting his stomach.

'Well, you've been gone a while.'

As lunch progressed Jana felt a pang of homesickness, and

in that moment she desperately wanted to be at home, to sit in the kitchen and chat to her mother about her week. Happiness eluded her in the most unexpected moments, and she tried to focus on other things to avoid the turmoil in her mind. Life in Letovice was good but very different from her familiar city life.

'That was tasty,' she said, watching Mrs Martinek scan the table.

'It's a pleasure. Who would like dessert?'

Miloš took some more, the others declined. He had been unusually quiet. By the evening Jana was grateful for her bed. It was strange to think of Miloš in another room in the house. Jana cast the thought aside and pulled the blankets over her head, blowing hot air down the sheets to warm up the bed. She lay in silence, listening to faint murmurs from the Martineks downstairs. Listening to their voices coming from beneath her room was comforting. It reminded her that she wasn't alone.

Chapter 5

Prague, November 1989

9 November 1989. A day nobody would forget. She had heard
rumours about the Wall. As they huddled around the television
screen in the apartment that evening, Jana's family looked on
in anticipation.

'Erich Honecker's prediction was wrong.'

'What's that, Tatínek?'

'He said the Berlin Wall would stay for another hundred
years. I knew he was wrong when I heard him say the words.
Dreaming, he was. Times are changing, my girl, and for the
better. You watch this.'

'Look,' said Irena, 'people are flooding through the
checkpoints into West Berlin.' The television screen flickered,
casting intermittent shadows across the walls of their living

room.

'I could feel it, even before the demonstrations broke out,' said her father. 'I knew it would be the end, or the beginning. Depends which way you look at it.'

The month before, refugees from East Germany had already begun making their way across the border into Czechoslovakia. Tatínek had predicted then that the wall would fall. He often made these almost prophetic announcements. It was eerie. He was still talking.

She knelt on the floor in front of Tatínek. He was leaning forward, making arm gestures and raising his eyebrows. His chest was rattling. It was always rattling these days.

'Twenty-eight years, and the people have finally escaped. They look like cattle. It's insanity – you can't keep control like this for ever. We've talked about it for long enough.' His fists pressed down into the arms of the chair. His eyes, wide and intense.

'Don't get so emotional, my love,' said Matka. 'It's not good for your health.'

She whisked away his ashtray as he started to cough.

'It's OK, just my lungs. That was my last cigarette of the evening.'

'I should think so. Let me get you some tea.'

'People are waiting to greet them on the other side,' said Aleš, joining in the conversation. 'Look at the graffiti.' He was leaning on the end of the sofa with his feet curled up next to Matka and Irena. He didn't often watch all the news, but this evening everyone was gripped. The phone rang.

'Yes, who is it? We're watching. *Dobrý*. Good. Talk tomorrow.'

Tatínek put the phone down as quickly as he had picked it up.

'Just a colleague. Guess everyone's watching but he wanted to check we'd seen the news.'

They watched the scene unfold in minute detail. As the young man smashed through the wall he was sprayed with a water cannon from the other side. Jana could see the dark uniforms through the hole in the wall. The scene carved itself into her mind. The images were to stay with her for a long time. You never know which events or images will remain with you until you look back, but this was one such moment. People in the West were chiselling away at the wall, some watching, waiting, many holding champagne, flowers, bananas – items which hadn't been available to the East Germans.

Irena and Aleš were fighting over the last piece of cake, Matka was rushing in and out of the kitchen with cups of tea and Tatínek was talking incessantly.

For the first time, Jana didn't really want to hear what he had to say. She wanted to absorb the details for herself and to reflect on what she knew would be a momentous occasion. Then make up her own mind.

They didn't know that their father would not be around the following June to see the official dismantling of the wall by German military. He was keen for a complete end to the division between East and West. It was something Jana didn't fully understand at the time.

Change wasn't always a good thing.

Eight days later, it was Friday 17 November 1989. Jana's father took her to join the crowds.

'I don't think this is a good idea, Tatínek.'

'Jana, this is important. It is time to rise up, take a stand. My students need the support. They're all marching, and I'm the one who's been encouraging them to stand up to all of this. I stand against it too – this madness of a government. I do not want you growing up with what I had, Jana. I want more for you, and for that I will fight.'

He held up his flag in a sea of red, white and blue. The blue arrow of the Czech flag pierced through the red and white.

'I'm afraid, Tatínek.'

He wrapped his arm around her and kissed her on the cheek.

'I love you, sweet girl. Don't ever let anyone tell you that things can't be changed, that things can't be done. They can and they will, if we are united in what we believe.'

They marched through the cold late afternoon air along Albertov towards the Vyšehrad Cemetery. The crowds gathered with students from all over Prague. It was International Students' Day, and spirits were high. The crowds chanted and raised their flags and banners.

'Opeltal, Opeltal.' The name reverberated through the atmosphere.

'I think the anniversary of his death has given them more of a reason to protest.' Tatínek scanned the crowds walking with them. He sometimes spoke in riddles that she didn't follow.

'Anniversary?'

'A student, Jan Opeltal – he was killed fifty years ago today when the Germans occupied Prague, during the war. I think people have had enough.'

'There were protests in Bratislava last night, weren't there?' Jana had seen the news.

'Yes, they ended peacefully. Hopefully this, too, will be a peaceful opposition, a silent voice. I don't want blood on my hands, I want justice.'

'You really believe that this works?'

'I want freedom for our country, for you, for Irena and for Aleš. I want you to grow up in a place where your words won't have to be stifled, for your generation to know freedom of speech. I've tried to fight the system alone but you can't, not if you're labelled a dissident …'

His words tailed off as he saw a young man running towards him. Jana wasn't sure what a dissident might be.

'Sir, this is it. This is what you've been talking about – the people, rising up to fight against the system. Stand up for what you believe in, is what you've always said. Well, I am, and I will. Thank you, thank you.'

Tatínek blushed. 'Don't thank me. Keep walking, and don't give up. Keep protesting until we have a democracy. I'm here until I see change.'

Jana watched the man shake hands with her father and embrace him, before he slipped back into the crowds. People were marching silently. A sea of colours, flags and banners.

Much like a carnival dragon, it heaved and moved, powered by people, without a word. Many of the banners had the word 'nonviolence' splashed across them in crude capitals on sheets of fabric. The words shouted in silence.

'One of your students, Tatínek?'

'Yes, yes. Here, take this.'

He dug into the inside pocket of his jacket with his free arm, and handed her a small gold locket. Jana cupped her hands and looked up at Tatínek. The crowd travelled past them. She noticed that they had stopped walking. People were shouting accusations about the government, and cheering. She could hear the word 'resign' repeated with increasing volume.

'It was my mother's. I've had it since she died. The only time I was without it was when I was inside. Your mother had it then.' He was quiet for a moment. 'I want you to have it. When you look at it, remember who you are, and that I love you.'

'Tatínek, we're not going to die, are we?' A baby in a pram passed them, pushed by a triumphant looking mother, waving her free arm in the air. The baby sat up with a white wool hat, mesmerised by the crowds.

He laughed, 'No, my sweet. I just want you to hold on to it. Maybe it'll bring you luck. There's no chain, but we'll get you one. My mother wore it every day, her mother before that. Come on, let's keep moving.'

They walked past the botanical gardens and along the Vlatva River. As the sun lowered into the city's skyline, casting an orange glow over the islands, Jana could feel people's hopes rising, rising above the fear and the oppression that Tatínek so often talked about. The chanting began like a war cry.

They walked over the rough cobbles and the tram tracks, and turned right on to Narodni Street by the National Theatre, an imposing building on the corner where the two streets met. Actors and actresses leaned out of the windows towards the river, waving and signing 'V for victory'. It was getting darker and colder but the atmosphere was alive, and she knew this, too, would make its mark in her memory.

'The police. Tatínek, it's the police.'

'Don't be afraid. We're not doing anything wrong. Keep walking.'

People held flowers up towards rows of armed police. Waves of carnations were lined up against transparent police shields.

'These shields are ironic.'

'What do you mean, Tatínek?'

'The government has been anything but transparent, and now they are using transparency to protect themselves.'

'I don't understand.'

The police had surrounded them and were starting to beat people, selecting individuals from the crowds. Tanks arrived, spraying the crowd with water cannons.

'Come, Jana, let's go.'

'But you said we would stay to the end.'

'It's not safe.'

He took her arm, and led her away down a side street. As

she turned back the crowd had dispersed. One man lay motionless on the street.

Some weeks later she heard the words 'velvet revolution'. She had worn a velvet dress once as a girl, deep crimson. Her father started to talk about how the teaching of 'Marxism-Leninism' and the history of the international workers' movement had all officially been removed from the curricula in universities and colleges. Were these the changes that they had marched for? What else would change? It was difficult to know what was safe. Nothing had felt safe to her since the day they first took Tatínek, she wasn't sure if it ever would. As people's hopes soared, Jana felt a tinge of fear. It was a fear that was set to stay for some time. She felt a traitor to the national mood – the adrenaline of change, the elation of hope.

Chapter 6

Letovice, June 1993

There was just enough time to phone home before her date. She knew it was important. Jana's mother answered with a breathless voice.

'Hello, my love, how are you?'

'Good, thanks. Busy week. Are you OK, Matka?'

'Yes, I'm just trying to get everything ready for your sister's wedding. When you add all the names together and look at the guest list it's daunting. Irena wants a small wedding. It's difficult to find a dress to hire that will fit her. She's too thin.'

'She's fine, Matka. Everyone hires dresses for their wedding day, don't they? There must be so many places in the city.'

'I just want her to enjoy the day, I want her to be happy, I want you all to be happy.' Her voice faded. These were words that Tatínek used to use.

'Look,' said Jana. 'I'll be home soon and I can help. Make me a list and I'll work my way through it when I get there, OK? Try not to worry, It's going to be a good day, I promise. We'll all be there. It will be fine, you'll see.'

'All right, my love. You sound tired, are you working too hard?'

The curious thing about mothers is that they know everything. Just from observing or hearing your voice they can tell what has been going on. They have a knack of teasing things out.

'Oh, it's just been a busy week. The Martineks have been kind letting me stay, so I'm doing what I can to help.'

'They seem like a nice family.'

'They are, Kamila's grandmother likes me to read to her. I'm doing my best.' Her best never felt good enough. She always felt that people wanted more from her. Jana deliberately avoided mentioning Miloš, just in case her mother started probing.

'That's my girl. I didn't bring you up just to think of yourself.'

'Good to hear you, Matka. I really should go now.'

Jana ended the conversation and put the phone down, not wanting to admit that she missed her family. Uncertainty over her future had taken root in her mind, and refused to move. Then there was Miloš. She had to get ready.

49

Looking at her small chest of drawers, Jana couldn't work out whether to wear something dressy or casual. She didn't want him to think that she was making too much of an effort. He might guess that she liked him. It was difficult to imagine that he liked her.

She reached for the red dress hanging on the back of the door. She grinned and swung it over her head, slipping her arms in through the delicate shoulders. A colleague had given it to her, in the hope that she would learn to wear something other than trousers. This would show off her figure, hidden under the perpetual winter layers. Looking into the mirror, she couldn't recall whether he had ever seen her in a dress.

Jana knew the outfit would be a hit because she felt good in it. Didn't every guy like a girl in a dress? How did she know what they liked? Smiling at her reflection, she added a smattering of lipstick, let her hair down and sauntered down the stairs.

Miloš was waiting in the living room. His parents were busy in the kitchen and hadn't noticed either of them.

'Wow'

'Do you like it?' She knew he did from the expression in his eyes.

'Like it? You look amazing. I'm not sure if I'm smart enough to take you out looking like this.'

Miloš looked good in his blue shirt. He was wearing a subtle amount of aftershave, which made him seem more masculine, and he had done something to his hair. Noticing her look, he ruffled it quickly.

'Oh, just a little wax.'

'I like it.' She smiled. 'You look good too.'

'Shall we?' He stood up and mischievously held out his arm, as if they were about to glide on to a dance floor and begin a waltz.

'Absolutely,' said Jana. She took his arm and they spun across the floor.

Clattering sounds echoed from the kitchen. They broke their waltz and ran into the hallway to find their coats. Miloš held Jana's coat up for her. His gesture surprised her. This was not the same boy who had forced snow down her back. He was different now – keener, more nervous.

Later in the evening they left the cinema. They had been able to sit together, alone, away from prying eyes. Miloš took her to the café in Letovice. His organization hadn't surprised her, but his nerves were out of character.

They stepped in through the doorway of the café at the bottom of the hill. Wine bottles were roughly stacked in an alcove in the wall with a guitar hanging to one side. He led the way across the tiled floor to a table at the back of the room. The square table sat neatly at an angle to the wall. Covered in orange tablecloths, each one had a small fabric flower arrangement in the middle. She could smell the beer mixed with the aroma of meat coming from the kitchen.

'People talk. Everyone knows everyone here. I thought you might like a quiet table.' Miloš pulled a chair out for her to sit down. She giggled and clutched her purse.

'In the city nobody knows anybody, and it doesn't matter

where you go. Are we hiding from someone?' She looked around the room.

A waiter appeared at their table. 'Would you like some wine, sir?' He stood wide-eyed and expectant. 'Miloš? It's Miloš, isn't it?'

'Yes, you look familiar.'

'We went to school together. I'm Tomas. I was in the year below you. I leave this summer.'

Jana looked at the collection of spirits in bottles lined up on the shelves above the bar, and glanced at the menu. Her appetite had vanished somewhere during the waltz.

They ordered food and Miloš's new friend offered them wine.

'I would suggest you try the Moravian Rulander. It's from the Znojmo vineyard, it's light.'

'That sounds good, thanks.' He nodded to Miloš and left.

'So, how have you enjoyed your time here?' Miloš used a mock interview voice.

Jana drew breath and smoothed the napkin, stroking it, as if she hoped it would soothe her nerves.

'It's been wonderful.' She smiled, unable to take her eyes away from the napkin. The waiter returned with the recommended bottle. He poured it into Miloš's glass and waited.

'A good choice.' Miloš nodded. 'Thank you.' The waiter quickly filled their glasses and scurried off to the other tables, which were now filling up.

'You don't talk about your father,' said Miloš. 'What is he

like?'

Jana went pale and spluttered, almost spitting out the wine.

'What's wrong?'

There was a long, awkward silence and she could feel herself struggling to keep her composure. A tear rolled down her cheek. Miloš wiped it away gently and held her hand. He was warm and comforting. His responses surprised her.

'What is it? Was he unkind to you?' He looked at her and waited.

'No, no. I…he…'

'It's OK, you don't have to tell me.'

'I've been wanting to tell you. I don't know why I haven't. He died three years ago. He caught pneumonia and became weak. His health wasn't good, but he got even weaker, then we lost him.'

His face dropped and he reached out for her other hand.

'To be honest, I haven't talked about it to anybody. At least not here. I thought that coming to Letovice would be a fresh start – nobody would make me talk about him.'

'Why didn't you just say?'

'I don't know really. I think I got used to not talking about it, about him. It was too much to cope with at the time and the family needed me to be strong for them. Now I don't know how I feel. Empty.'

'Oh, Jana. I'm so sorry. I've been teasing you and messing around, and now you tell me this. I'm a fool.'

She raised her eyes and looked at him with surprise. She sat there in her beautiful red dress with a tear-stained face. He stroked her cheek, and cupped her chin with his hand. This was the gentle side to him that she had seen occasional glimpses of when he was with Babička. It made her feel peaceful, not a feeling she was familiar with. She looked up at him.

'I hadn't planned to tell anyone. It just slipped out. You ask too many questions.'

'Sorry. I just hate to see you struggling.'

'I'm OK, really.' She shook her head.

'You always seem to be so strong.'

'I'm not, Miloš. I just try to be. Not very successfully, either. I just have moments of not feeling so strong. That's all. We all do, don't we?'

'It's all right. You don't need to explain. I understand.'

Jana liked the way he stroked her hair. Tatínek stroked her hair when she was younger, before she went to sleep. The waiter arrived with their plates and disappeared just as quickly through the kitchen doors and into the steam.

'So what happened? To your father, I mean?'

Jana drew a short breath. 'His health had been bad since…since his days inside.'

'Inside?' Miloš's eyes widened.

'I'm not really sure, but Matka says he was writing things that the state didn't like, something to do with his work. We never really talked about it. He said he didn't want us to get caught up in it.' She saw his expression. 'He was innocent.'

'I'm so sorry, Jana.'

'It's OK, there was nothing anyone could do.' She tried to

brush the uncomfortable thoughts to one side.

'What did he do?' said Miloš tentatively.

'He was a lecturer at the University of Political and Economic Sciences in Prague. I think he should have been a teacher. He was great with us when we were younger; children loved him, everyone did.'

Jana felt her breathing becoming progressively shallower. Her legs felt weak. She gripped the table.

'They took him away when I was six.'

'Who did?'

Jana realised that Miloš probably had not experienced the horrors that many in Prague had endured. Why would he? He did not have any political connections that she knew of.

'The secret police.' She took a swift gulp of wine and sat back.

'What happened?' Miloš leaned forwards.

'He was in prison on and off throughout my childhood. I was there, I was there when they first took him away. Matka didn't know that I'd seen, it was some time before sunrise. I'll never forget the look in his eyes, it was as if he knew they would come.'

'And you've never told this to anyone?' His face looked pained.

She shook her head. 'I can still remember them searching through his things, it was horrible.' Jana clasped her mouth.

'It's OK.' He stroked her hand. 'Take your time.'

'I couldn't bring myself to ask Matka why they had taken him. She pretended that he'd gone away on business. I pretended I knew nothing. My brother and sister believed the lie. There were so many lies that we had to live with…and secrets. It was only when he was first released that he told me. He said he had to fight for the truth.'

'Did he give you a reason?' Miloš looked earnest and sad – sad for her loss, maybe.

'He had economics degrees and doctorates to his name, but his real passion was politics. He said it was his political views that got him into trouble.'

Miloš poured her another glass, without breaking his gaze.

'He refused to teach from the required curriculum. He was always stubborn – 'principled,' he called it.'

'I can understand that. He must have been a strong man, your father. To survive prison must have been…I don't know what it must have been like but I know it takes courage to stand up for what you believe in, in the face of persecution.'

She forced a smile and twirled a few strands of hair between her fingers. 'He had already had some close shaves by then. Tatínek didn't want to lose his job or jeopardise the security of his family.'

'But they got to him in the end.' Miloš said it in a way that could be interpreted as a question or a statement.

'Yes, several times. No sooner was he released than they caught him again and reeled him in. There was always a reason. It was endless. He came and went over the years. He was brave – fearless. I don't feel so brave. I spent so much of my childhood living in fear – fear of him being taken away again, fear of losing the people I loved.' She glanced across the room. 'One of his friends had written a book that was banned for allegedly promoting too many Western ideologies. It was something that they sat on, hard. He learned to tread carefully, but he wasn't careful enough.'

'I can't imagine what it must have been like for you as a child.' His voice sounded softer. 'We heard stories, of course, but I didn't know anyone who had actually been persecuted. I know that some people lost their jobs and places in schools for their children, even their homes.'

'There were good times before he died.' She forced herself to remember the good moments. 'His enthusiasm was infectious. I remember him talking about different leaders and theories. I soaked up all of his tales. He was a good storyteller. I think I was his outlet for all the things that he hadn't been allowed to say publicly. He taught his students, but only trusted a few with his 'truths,' as he called them.'

'You need to hold on to those memories.'

'We marched, you know, on the first day of the revolution.'

'Really? Weren't you a bit young?'

'That's how persuasive he was. I was there before I had time to think about it, marching, waving my flag, our flag.'

He looked impressed. 'So, am I dating a revolutionary?'

'Let's not get carried away,' she said. 'Is this a date?'

He laughed. 'I hope so.'

She didn't know how to respond. 'So, following the revolution...'

'Which you started.'

'Don't be ridiculous.'

'It's a thought, though.'

'Yes, but it's not the truth. The truth is that I felt more like a spectator. The students were so passionate. You could feel it, the frustration. There was a fire in their eyes. After the revolution the university was reorganised, and Tatínek was heavily involved in the planning process. He was a well-respected man, and very capable.' She hesitated. 'I haven't spoken his name for a long time.'

'Jana, you're beautiful.'

'What?'

'I said, you're beautiful.'

She had heard him properly the first time. Her thoughts were cut short, as he leant forward and kissed her. It was a passionate kiss that took her by surprise. She felt a rush of excitement for the first time since that day in the streets.

Friday evening arrived too quickly. The Martinek family bustled around Jana, rushing to answer the door to relatives and pulling food out of the oven. It looked more like a Greek family wedding than a send-off. Mrs Martinek had gone to great lengths to make it a special occasion.

Jana wondered whether Mrs Martinek thought she was leaving Letovice and never returning. Friends and extended family started to arrive in what felt like droves. The events of the previous weekend had left Jana reluctant to leave Letovice and Miloš, but Irena needed her there for the wedding.

'Jana, my love,' said Mrs Martinek's sister. 'Come here, let me see you.'

A large lady, with a larger-than-life outlook, Jana hadn't seen her since arriving in Letovice six months previously. She remembered how much the larger-than-life lady could talk. She was an expert on every subject and, if you had been somewhere, she had been there countless times. If you had experienced something exciting she would go one better and describe it in even greater, more elaborate detail.

'What has the country air done for you? You look a little pale. Are you all right?' She clasped Jana's forehead with one hand and waved the other in the air. She waved at least one arm in the air every time she spoke.

'Oh, you do still look lovely, though, doesn't she, Miloš?' He stood behind the larger-than-life lady, and opened his mouth to respond.

The larger-than-life lady scanned the room. 'Where is that sister of mine? I have something for her. Where are all these people coming from?'

She rushed into the kitchen before anyone could answer her questions, or catch the crimson colour rising in Jana's cheeks.

They smiled at each other knowingly, and Miloš shot glances in her direction throughout the evening, without anybody noticing. He used the occasional hand gesture – a swift movement of a forefinger across the throat, a roll of the eyes. It was a silent conversation between the two of them below the rise of voices from across the room.

The larger-than-life lady had brought her two small children and her husband, who was considerably quieter. The room filled up with people and children flew around the house in circuits. The Martineks' house had a hallway, which led into the kitchen, and you could walk through the kitchen to the living room and back out into the hall. It was perfect for chasing in circles.

This was the first time she had experienced the house full of children. All these people, here to say farewell. She felt honoured.

As they ate Jana thought about the way she had felt the other evening, when he had kissed her. She looked across at him chatting with his five-year-old nephew. The little boy appeared to be fascinated by the lace place mats on the table, folding and unfolding each one, like the flaps of an envelope. Miloš was gentle with him. He listened carefully, copying the boy's movements and allowing him to talk and to ask questions.

Mr Martinek got up to pour more drinks and offered the adults his favourite tipple.

'Becherovka,' he announced, handing Jana a shot glass. 'Drink up.'

It had been her father's favourite drink on special occasions, and Mr Martinek offered it with the same sense of pride. Jana took a sip, she could taste the aniseed, cinnamon, and a mixture of herbs. All eyes turned towards her.

'Don't drink it like that, girl, take it all in one go.' He laughed, and his whole body shook. Miloš smirked from the other side of the room, and Mrs Martinek looked concerned.

'Don't force her, miláčku.'

He glanced at his wife, and continued to chuckle. 'Why

not? Looks as though she might need it.' He looked at Miloš, who turned away.

Babička raised an empty hand towards Jana, her head bobbing up and down in agreement with her son-in-law. She sat in a reclining chair in the corner of the room under one of her husband's paintings. She liked to sit close to his work; she said it made her feel near to him.

Mr Martinek turned back to Jana. 'Thirty-eight per cent alcohol, sixty-two per cent fire – all the way from Karlovy Vary. I give it to Babička sometimes. Helps with the arthritis, doesn't it?'

She bobbed her head and smiled in a way that made the lines around her lips almost disappear. Her face lit up in recognition. Some of the other faces in the room smiled, others grimaced.

'It'll help your indigestion and wipe away your cares.'

Jana took the advice, against her better judgement, and felt the liquid burn as it reached the back of her throat and rolled down into the pit of her stomach. The fire coursed through her body and temporarily paralysed her lungs. She held her breath.

'Well?' said Mr Martinek.

Jana breathed in deeply and nodded, unable to speak until the fire had subsided. She held her chest, and gasped.

'It's…it's different.'

He looked surprised. 'Ha. Different? It's the best there is.'

His pride and joy in the form of this national spirit was going to take some getting used to. If, indeed, she even wanted to get used to something that set fire to your insides.

'Thank you.' She forced the words out.

'It's all right. I just wanted you to try it. Miloš told me you've never had it before.

Miloš shrugged, and held his hands up. It felt like some kind of an initiation ceremony into the Martinek household. Jana hadn't seen Mr Martinek this animated, and she suspected he had started drinking the fire juice before the official toasts. What else had Miloš told him about her?

'Here's to Jana, her safe return to us, and to her sister and her husband-to-be.'

They all raised a glass. Babička now had a full glass in her hand.

'To Jana.' Resounding cheers followed the toast, and Jana wondered why he was so keen for her to return to Letovice, to them. Maybe just to drink the fire juice and become a proper Czech.

'Miloš, are you OK?' said Kamila. 'You seem preoccupied.' His sister spoke quietly, with her body turned away from the crowded room. People started to clear plates from the table.

'Yes,' he said. 'Just tired, I think. I've been studying until late into the night and I'm struggling to form any kind of intelligent conversation. It's nothing really, don't worry.' She poured him another drink, and looked over at Jana.

As the evening drew to a close, Jana thanked the Martineks for their kindness in arranging the meal. Miloš quickly offered to take her to the station the following morning. Jana was surprised, but pleased that he wanted to take her. She needed time alone with him before she left, and it would have been hard for her to say goodbye to him with the rest of the family.

Fortunately, the others didn't offer to join them, and she decided to go to bed as soon as they had washed up. Not wanting to drag out the rest of the evening, she kissed them all and headed upstairs to the safety of her room. She had tried to stop herself from kissing Miloš on the lips. Jana hoped he wasn't offended. Feeling as though she had to behave normally around him, she had tried to keep a distance.

As she closed her bedroom door the red dress swung from side to side, as if it was dancing. Details of the other evening flooded her mind. She felt a rush of excitement at what had happened, and she fell into her bed wondering what tomorrow morning would hold. Would he kiss her again? How would she survive the summer without him? It was the last time that she would hear the Martineks downstairs for a while. She eventually drifted off to sleep.

The morning began with a rushed breakfast. They were all sad to see her go, and told her to write to them, or phone if she could. Jana checked her suitcase to see if she had everything, and Miloš loaded it into the family car. They all kissed her goodbye. Babička pulled her forwards and kissed her on the forehead. Kamila blew kisses from the front door as they drove down the road.

Jana knew that she would miss Letovice, it was a beautiful place. She loved the Drahanska Vrchovina hills, the view of the castle and the monastery, and would miss looking at the rooftops as she walked down into the town.

'Will you write?' Miloš asked.

'Yes, of course. I'll tell you all about the wedding.'

'I'm sure your sister will be pleased to have you back at home. Everyone will.'

They pulled up at the station, avoiding any further conversation. Miloš carried her bag to the platform and squeezed her tightly. Jana breathed in his scent. It would have to last until she returned.

She could feel his heart beating rapidly. They had said all they needed to, for now. He let her go slowly as the train approached, holding onto her hand until she pulled away and boarded the train. She watched him waiting on the platform. He looked lost. He never looked lost. Her heart sank as she tried not to think of this as another loss, just a temporary separation.

Remembering how she had counted backwards from twenty as a girl, when thoughts of Tatínek weighed heavily on her mind in his absence, she tried it again. This time the sinking feeling refused to leave. She traced the shape of his outline on the window as the train pulled away from the station. His image pulled away and disappeared out of view.

Chapter 7

The rhythm of the train, on its journey towards Prague, lulled Jana into a sleepy haze. The soporific sound of the wheels clunking on the tracks below slowed her whirling thoughts to a smooth diminuendo. She closed her eyes for a moment, feeling herself relax.

She woke as the ticket collector appeared. Looking at her watch, the past hour appeared to have vanished, along with the, now familiar, Blansko landscape. Glancing out of the window, the sunlight caught the ripples of the Moravian mountains. The hills dipped into pockets of trees and vineyards. Scenes much like the painting in the Martineks' home filled her line of vision.

Jana wondered what Havel would do to protect their country. It was vulnerable to outside influence now that the tight restrictions had released their grip. She remembered her father speaking fondly of their president, Václav Havel, who was also from her beautiful city of Prague. He had had the unique experience of being the last president of Czechoslovakia and the first president of the Czech Republic. He led Czechoslovakia until last year, when he resigned – on 20 July – after the Slovaks issued their Declaration of Independence. He had recently been re-elected as the first president of the new Czech Republic, in January 1993, the same month that she had left Prague for Letovice. He believed that the salvation of the world lay in the heart.

Jana wondered where her heart would lead her if she let it run free. It had been broken through such a deep loss and now, in a smaller way, she was losing Miloš. Although only a temporary separation, it felt like yet another wrench from safety, another anchor pulled up out of the water.

Jana never understood people's fascination with Havel, a man who – according to her father – had supported neither socialism nor capitalism. Instead he proclaimed a so-called 'third way'. Was he just being lured by the idea of westernising the Czech Republic? He had been a passionate supporter of non-violent resistance, a role in which he had been compared, by President Bill Clinton, to Mahatma Gandhi and Nelson Mandela.

She thought about his influence during the 1989 revolution, just before her father died. Having brought an end to communism, maybe they had opened themselves up to trouble of another kind.

Jana remembered Tatínek being away for some months

when she was a girl and, as she grew older, he began to tell her of his meeting with Havel. Both had been imprisoned for their anti-Soviet activities – Jana's father for teaching his students too much about the Western economy, and Havel for bringing the world's attention to the Czechoslovakian 'struggle', as they called it.

Havel was born into an intellectual family, his mother was the daughter of a journalist and an ambassador. She encouraged his artistic ambitions and he became a playwright. Because of his work he was denied access to university and attended the Faculty of Economics at the Czech Technical University, where he had had a brief encounter with Jana's father.

Havel had his passport confiscated in 1967 because his writings were considered to be too subversive. Before his imprisonment he had been hounded by the police and repeatedly arrested for being a threat to the republic and working against the Communist regime. He had been offered the chance to emigrate but he chose imprisonment. Havel was hugely influenced by the works of Kafka, which had been almost buried by the authorities.

Jana had always wondered what it was that drove this man to the point that he would actually choose to go to prison rather than to escape. What great conviction he must have had in his own mind about where the country needed to go, its political direction. She almost envied his determination and grit, even if she wasn't completely sure of his motives and beliefs.

Jana's father talked for hours about Havel's relentless battle against the state. He had apparently co-founded a human rights movement, Charter 77, and some other committee, to defend those who were persecuted. That's what those papers were about, the papers the men were waving on the morning that Tatínek was taken away. He had later explained to her that Havel's mission was to restore democracy in their country, and that he, too, believed strongly in a democratic society.

Jana wasn't sure what she really thought about democracy. She only knew that where there was tension in a person's life or country it was difficult to feel a real sense of freedom. As people around her were feeling liberated after the recent fall of communism, Jana was fearful of the future, both for the Czech Republic and for her own life. She felt uncertain about so many things, and this was made all the more difficult because she couldn't talk to Tatínek. Although Jana didn't always agree with his views she respected him and valued his judgement. She missed him deeply and it left her feeling alone.

Looking out of the carriage she recognised the distinctive Bohemian landscape. It was a land of baroque castles and stunning scenery along the Vltava and Sazava rivers. The mountains were beautiful and the forests stretched out for miles. The Krkonose National Park lay just northwest of Prague. Jana longed to see it. Much of that area was untouched and unspoilt. She also wanted to visit the well known hot mineral springs in Karlovy Vary, beyond Prague – the land of the fire juice.

Jana had heard that people such as Freud, Marx and Goethe had visited the springs, and she wanted to go and see them for herself.

Now that they had left Moravia behind, the scenery was more dramatic. They were drawing near to Prague, and she felt a tingle of excitement at the thought of seeing her mother and the rest of her family and friends. Jana soaked up the view of the Prazskt Hrad Castle at Hradčany Square in the distance, with the spires of St. Vitus' Cathedral rising up out of the centre of the castle. The contrasting architecture made it look like an elaborate film set. Tatínek had taken her there so often as a young girl. It reminded her of his enthusiasm over the history of the buildings.

He used to tell her about the sieges, fires and floods that had previously destroyed so many of the castles and palaces. She remembered him talking to her in great depth about the disastrous fire of 1541, which destroyed the whole of Hradčany itself. He thought the resulting Renaissance and baroque interiors of today's palace were worth taking over a century to build, he loved the fine detail and the grandeur of it all. The Austrian Empress, Maria Theresa, had ordered its reconstruction in the 1700s, and the result was magnificent.

Towering over the city, it was, her father had boasted, the largest castle in the world. As it stood at 1870 feet long and 426 feet wide she could believe he was right, and wondered whether it was listed in any record books. Jana had been afraid of the fighting giants on either side of the entrance as a child. They dwarfed the guards below and she imagined that one day they would leap out of their intimidating positions and run after people. The guards would not have been strong enough to overpower them.

She was intrigued by the round Mihulka Tower, or Powder Tower, at the northern end of the castle. It had been a place where alchemists were once employed to elicit the secret of turning base metals into gold. It had always sounded mysterious and exciting. It was turned into a gunpowder storehouse, but Jana ignored this part of the story and imagined what might have gone on in the tower many years before she had been born. She pictured guards looking out over the city, protecting it from siege, or lovers scaling the walls to reach the objects of their affection.

The cathedral was much older, having taken nearly six centuries to build, and this was the part that she fell in love with each time she walked inside, captivated by it's light and the grandeur. It stood on the site of a chapel founded in 925. As a girl, with a limited understanding of time, Jana had wondered how long six centuries would take to live through. It was difficult when you were only ten years old to grasp this kind of time frame. It was over sixty times her age.

The breath-taking stained-glass windows were unlike any she had ever seen. Through the intensity of the sun, their colours cast hues of blue, red and yellow onto the stone pillars, giving a burst of colour to the inside of the cathedral. The chapel of St Wenceslas, one of the oldest parts of the building, had walls encrusted with jasper and amethyst.

The frescos depicted scenes from the passion of Christ, and she wondered if it was anything like the Sistine Chapel, which she had read about. The coronations of all their past kings and queens here, in this building, must have been an awe-inspiring sight. This sublime beauty was almost hidden within the castle walls. She believed that the treasured things in life were often hard to find – a pearl in an oyster shell, a kind word in the heat of the moment.

Another treasure place was Golden Lane, behind the cathedral. Jana liked to be able to wander freely down this alluring and enchanting street. It had been built against the interior of the castle walls for the archers of the Castle Guard, but had apparently deteriorated by the time Kafka moved into number twenty-two. Jana wondered whether this row of colourful, almost miniature, cottages would change and eventually be turned into a tourist attraction, gated with an admission charge, spoilt. She hoped it would be protected from the changing times, which loomed over the horizon.

She breathed in the scent of summer bloom through the open window. The city was beguiling.

As the train pulled into Hlavni Nadrazi station, Jana thought about what lay ahead for the summer break. The excitement of her sister's wedding had escaped her in recent months, and now it was only a week away. What would it be like to see her family again? With mixed feelings, she pulled the large travel bag on to her shoulder and stepped out of the carriage onto the platform. Her mother, brother and sister were standing at the station, waiting.

'Jana. Welcome home.'

Irena ran towards her. The stress of the wedding was evident in her eyes, and there appeared to be less of her than before, if that were possible. Jana stopped for a moment as she briefly saw her father's expression in her sister's eyes. She didn't know if it was comforting or unnerving. Maybe she was just searching for anything that reminded her of him.

'You look lovely. You must be so excited about the wedding,' she said, realizing her sister needed some encouragement.

'I am. Well, I will be once we get there. I'm so tired.'

'I'm sure. It's good to see you all again, and to be home.'

Matka and Aleš, grabbed both girls. They stayed in a huddle on the platform for longer than she had anticipated. People sprinted past them, heading towards the exit. The train began to pull away, moving slowly out of the station. Aleš had never been keen on hugs or any kind of affection. It was good to see them. Everything felt normal again, and she could smell her mother's perfume. It reminded her of her childhood. She had worn the same scent for as long as they could remember, a warm musk.

'It's good to have you home,' said Aleš.

'How is everyone?' asked Jana.

'Let's get back and have some coffee,' said Matka, 'and we can catch up properly.'

'OK,' Jana looked at Aleš and smiled.

'Let me take your bag,' he said, 'it must be heavy.'

'Thanks. How have you been?'

'Good, just a lot of revision and papers to write.'

'You must be looking forward to the summer.'

Jana knew that Aleš was dealing with all the bills and

paperwork. Matka was not the most organised person, and hated going through this kind of thing. When Tatínek had died Aleš was expected to organise everything and tie up all the loose ends. She imagined that he had also been called upon to calm any frayed nerves in the run-up to the wedding. He appeared to have grown into his father's shoes.

'It's been frantic,' said Aleš. 'I escape for a beer every so often.' He smiled wryly and they exchanged glances. She understood.

'I can imagine. I wish I'd been there to help.'

'We've been fine, Jana,' Matka interrupted. 'Really, don't worry.' She was always listening in to every conversation, just in case she missed the smallest morsel of important information. 'You've only missed the chaos. It's good to have time now to see you before the big day.'

They strolled along the platform, as if there was not a care in the world, and headed slowly out towards the street. The large station clock reminded that time compressed itself when least expected. Jana wanted to savour the moment before it vanished, but Irena and Matka were only interested in getting home, with still so much to do.

The tram pulled in opposite the station exit, the light blinding them as they walked out on to the street. Matka stepped up into the carriage and found a seat near the back, followed by Jana. Aleš sat opposite them, and Irena shuffled into a place next to him. Tapping her feet on the wooden slats of the tram floor, Irena started to talk.

'You'll love my dress,' she said.

'You've got it?' said Jana.

'Yes, it's perfect, just not where I'd have expected to find it.'

'What do you mean?'

'Lida's grandmother lent me her dress.'

'Really? That's kind of her.'

'We were talking about it and she showed me her wedding dress and asked if I'd like to try it on. It was too big, at first, but she's good with a needle, and she's taken it in for me. It saved me having to hire one, and it's beautiful.'

Jana looked at Aleš. 'Have you seen it?' she asked.

'No, I'll wait for the day.'

'I suppose that's right.' She smiled. Jana could see that Aleš was not wildly interested in the dress.

'Tell me what it looks like,' said Jana, turning towards her sister.

'It's a simple dress with a top layer of lace. She made it herself for her wedding day and the lace fabric has buttons all the way down the back.'

'It sounds very elegant.'

'She covered the buttons herself. Lida and I thought it would be beautiful, and it meant so much that her grandmother had made it, and was willing to lend it to me.'

'I'm lending her my necklace from our wedding day,' said Matka. 'The one with a pearl on a chain.'

Irena was a few years older than Jana, and looked entirely different. She had dark hair and was tall and slim. Being a quieter character, she had always found it hard to get to know people, and never liked a fuss. Jana wasn't surprised that she wanted a small wedding. Her attention to detail made her a good lawyer Jana had wanted Irena's long dark hair and chocolate-coloured eyes. She was a stronger build than her sister, but shorter and less willowy.

Nobody would have guessed, on first glance, that they were related, although they had the same purposeful walk, and shared a few mannerisms. Their voices had a similar tone, which made them difficult to distinguish on the telephone, but their mother always knew which one was which. Jana thought it was appropriate for Irena to borrow a dress from her other bridesmaid's grandmother, and a necklace from their mother. It seemed more personal.

The tram lurched and juddered as it crossed points in the track. The buildings were just as she remembered them, tall and elegant. People bustled through the narrow streets in different directions. They passed the bakery, which Jana used to walk to with Matka as a young girl. The day was warm and fresh, and she wanted to get out and see Prague.

They jumped off at their tram stop and walked towards the building by the post office. They reached the front door and walked up the stairs. Jana breathe in the smell of musty wood and paint of the apartment block – it felt familiar. Their front door, on the first floor, had been repainted in a light brown nondescript colour. Matka turned the key in the lock and swung the door open.

'There,' she said. 'We're home, welcome back.'

The red cushion that she had made at school was still lying

on the sofa, and the family photographs were scattered around the living room. The dark wood cabinets showed off the ornaments, which her parents had collected over time. The rugs looked as though they had been freshly aired. The place was clean and welcoming. She could see her father's framed certificates still hanging in pride of place on the wall.

The photograph of Matka and Tatínek had been moved to the front of the cluster of pictures in the living room. Perhaps Matka had wanted a constant reminder of him, fearful that she might struggle to remember how he looked.

Jana knew that she would not have been able to look at a picture of him daily. It was all she could do to put him out of her mind, for the moment. The pain would break her if she allowed herself to think of him too often.

Drifting off to sleep that night, there wasn't the disturbing silence that she had expected. The trams clunked on the tracks outside, and she remembered counting each one as it passed when she was a younger. It helped her to sleep. Matka used the same washing powder on the sheets. The scent of her pillow brought back memories of Tatínek telling her stories at night.

The morning light pierced through the trees at the back of the building. She stood in her dressing gown, cupping a warm mug of coffee in her hands. Jana thought about how the swing that hung from the largest tree was beginning to look old and weathered. It had withstood years of abuse from the three of them but was still just as firmly attached to the branch. Jana remembered Aleš pushing her so high that she thought she would fly over the fence and into the next-door garden, although he never actually let her go any higher than the top of the fence. She remembered a time when he killed a wasp to stop it getting to Irena when she was small.

There was a knock at the door. Jana turned the handle hesitantly and a face on the other side of the door smiled. A man stepped forward and handed her a parcel.

'I wanted to come over to deliver this to Irena.'

'What is it?' She didn't know what to make of the tall stranger, or his mysterious gift.

'It's a wedding present for Irena.'

'Thank you.'

'Are you Jana?' the stranger asked her. How did he know who she was? There was something appealing about him, despite a dishevelled look. He was older than her with intriguing looks. He had a mass of brown hair, more facial hair than a day without a razor could create, and a scruffy blue shirt. His eyes were dark and intense. He must have noticed her concern.

'I'm sorry. I haven't introduced myself.' He offered her his hand. She hesitated.

'I went to school with Benes. I'm Lukas.'

'Good to meet you.'

'I can't make it to the wedding but I wanted to give them a present.'

'Do you want to come in?' she said, wanting him to stay so that she could find out more about him. Her curiosity had won.

'Thank you, but I can't stay.'

With that he turned and walked towards the stairs. Jana realised that she was still watching him and closed the door quickly.

There wasn't a sound in the apartment, maybe the others had gone out. Looking at the clock, she noticed that she must have got up late. Jana picked up her bridesmaid's dress from the table and started to sew the hem before time ran out. A friend had made both dresses, and Jana had wanted to wait until she was home to finish the length on her own dress.

Her thoughts turned to Miloš. She wished that he could meet her family. She knew he would like them, although her brother might have interrogated him. Jana thought she would be relieved to have time to herself, but this morning she didn't want to be alone. She found herself wishing that the man at the door had stayed a while longer. He was interesting, there was something slightly aloof and unobtainable about him. The Martineks' home in Letovice had been a daily hive of frenetic activity, but back in her family home, the silence was unwelcome.

She hung out the washing, then slumped into the large armchair in the corner of the living room. Looking at photos of their childhood made her wonder what life would throw into her path. It had been simple before the men came to take Tatínek away, but now there were so many decisions to make.

What if she made the wrong choices, or never felt fulfilled, never reached her potential? Jana wasn't sure if she wanted a family, she wasn't sure if she could protect a child from what she had experienced. Living up to the relationship her parents had would be difficult. They had had so much respect for each other. It was almost infuriating. No, she was steadily reaching the conclusion that the less change or risk she took, the easier life would be in the long run. She knew that Tatínek would be unimpressed but he never showed any fear. Whether or not he actually felt it, she would never know. She felt fear almost all the time. It was a fear of any situation she couldn't control. She would miss the old regime. Things were already starting to feel too uncertain.

Seeing Matka brought her comfort. There was nobody in the world that she felt more relaxed with, to be here right now was all she needed. She suddenly remembered the buns – the *kolache* buns that Matka had made needed to be delivered to the neighbours. Traditionally, they were given a few weeks before the wedding as an invitation to the reception, but there had been no time. Each one was filled with a different filling and beautifully wrapped.

It was a good opportunity for her to catch up with everyone in the street, and to greet them before the wedding day itself.

Nothing here had changed much, but everyone had been kept up to date with her news. The lady next door, Alicia, was a good friend of Matka's, and Jana knew that she had been a steady support for her, especially over the past few years. Alicia was so pleased to see Jana she almost knocked the *kolache* out of Jana's arms in her enthusiasm.

Alicia had watched them all grow up and she knew everything about the family. She was a neat lady with a broad grin, only half the height of Jana's brother. She always wore her hair up and came to the door in an apron. She baked every morning, the smell often tantalisingly seeping in through the window of their apartment. Alicia regularly brought Matka parcels of food. She squeezed Jana's cheeks.

'You look worried, my girl. Everything ok?'

'Yes, of course. It's the big day next week. How have they been and how are you, Alicia?'

'They're all well but they've missed you.'

'It's good to be back but it's strange without him.'

'I know, it will just take time to adjust. You had to shoulder a lot of the burden after he…when he died.'

Jana felt a sharp pain in her chest. 'I didn't do much,' she insisted.

'Yes, you did, my dear. You listened to your mother and you held everything together. It wasn't easy for you. Now it's your brother's turn.'

They looked at each other for a moment and Jana stroked Alicia's arm.

'Thank you, thank you for being here for her. I appreciate it. I didn't think I could go away, but it helped. At least, I think it did.'

'So, tell me all about Letovice. How was it? Here, have one of these.' Alicia pulled out a chair and handed Jana a hot bun. It was still steaming and it smelled deliciously of hot, sweet vanilla.

Jana sat on the edge of the seat and took a deep bite into the bun. 'These are good, Alicia.'

Alicia blushed. 'So,' she said, sounding resolute. 'Any

romance in the air?'

Jana squinted and decided to tell Alicia about him. 'I did meet someone, Miloš. He is the son of the family I stayed with.' It felt strange to talk about him.

'Ooh, sounds interesting.' Alicia sat down next to Jana and leaned into the table. 'Tell me more.'

'There's not much to say. He wants to be a doctor, he's bright and interested in lots of things, he listens. It's not every day that people really listen to what you say, Alicia. We got together just before I left but I won't see him for a while. Please, don't tell Matka. I don't want to complicate things. You know how she asks lots of questions.'

Alicia nodded. 'Your secret's safe with me, my dear.'

'Thank you.' Jana didn't want to tell her family about him just yet. There was too much else going on. They talked for a long time and Jana felt herself start to relax.

The wedding day approached with great speed and Irena woke them all up on Saturday morning, singing to herself and clattering in the kitchen. The four of them had breakfast and Lida arrived soon after they had finished. There were various phone calls from well-wishers who wouldn't be at the wedding, and the postman arrived with a flurry of cards.

'I can't breathe,' said Irena.

'Yes you can. Breathe slowly,' said Jana.

'Here's some water.' Aleš was two steps ahead and had already filled a glass. 'Try that. It should help.'

'Really, sweetheart,' said Matka, 'it's not that frightening.

You're marrying the person you want to be with and it's going to be an amazing day.' She tried to reassure her, but the look on Irena's face was unfamiliar to them all. She was normally so calm.

Her face crumpled, and tears began to wet her cheeks. Aleš placed a hand on her shoulder and they looked at her in silence.

'What is it? What's upsetting you?' Matka insisted.

'I miss him,' she said, 'I miss his …' Her voice tailed off.

'I know,' said Matka, 'we all do, but he would want you to be happy.'

'I just never thought he would miss this day.' She blew her nose, which was now glistening. They all looked at each other. Matka looked concerned.

'I just thought I'd be OK, but I don't know if I can go through with it.'

'What do you mean?' Jana asked.

'I don't know if I can do it without him.'

'Of course you can. we're all here for you, and Benes will be waiting at the church.'

'He promised me everything would be OK and that he'd be there for me.' Irena had not reacted when he died, Jana imagined this was a release for her.

'We're here,' said Aleš, trying to reassure her. When had he changed? He had grown up. 'It's going to be all right and he would want you to be happy. We all miss him, but you have to push through it.'

This was the first time Aleš had ever admitted their loss, or even mentioned their father. Jana hugged Irena tightly and tried to give her some kind of comfort. She watched Aleš intently to see if he was about to say more.

Irena looked up. 'Thank you,' she said. 'Thank you.'

Matka looked at her kindly and stroked her face. 'You look so much like him.'

'Really?'

'Yes, every time I look at you I see him.'

'I'm sorry. I didn't mean to wallow. It's just a big day.'

'We're all here for you and we love you,' said Jana. 'I'm giving you away,' said Aleš, 'so you'll have to hold on tightly. I'm not picking you up off the floor.'

They laughed, his humour always broke the uncomfortable moments. Jana could see how much he was changing, almost as though he had stepped into his father's shoes. She admired the way he was dealing with the situation.

How would things be without Tatínek? Jana knew Matka would need support and that the day would be tinged with grief. She hoped Irena would be so absorbed by the whole event that the pain would be eased by her excitement.

Jana approved of Benes, he was lucky to have her sister. Since the conversation a few months ago with Babička in her room, she had thought differently about marriage. She began to see it less as just a legal contract, realising that there was infinitely more to the intertwining of two lives than just the formalities.

Despite witnessing the closeness and trust in her parents' marriage as a child, something about the world around her had made Jana cynical. Marching in the crowds, watching strangers snatch Tatínek away from them – experiences like these had left her with a deep level of distrust in people. It was a disquieting pain that frequently stole her peace like a thief – uninvited, intruding, trespassing.

Somewhere deep in her soul she needed to find peace.

Chapter 8

Jana and Matka helped Irena into her dress. They fastened the buttons and handed her a simple bouquet of wild flowers. She looked frail but stunning. They walked into the hallway and left the apartment together, nobody said a word.

Arriving at the church, they saw local well-wishers. Aleš grinned as he saw her and nodded in the way that he did when he showed approval. He took Irena's trembling arm and led her slowly down the aisle towards the altar.

The church was full of flowers, heads slowly turned and people's faces lit up. The small children, mostly belonging to various friends and a niece of Benes, walked down the aisle in front of them, scattering petals. Irena wore a crown of rosemary given to her by her friends. She had almost forgotten it in the rush of the morning, but Jana had managed to put it in place just as they left the building.

The rosemary represented wisdom, love and loyalty, all of which were needed for the years ahead. The tiny roses softened the crown and made it look fresh. They matched the bridesmaids' dresses, which were only just pink. The girls looked like garden fairies from a book Jana had read as a child – ethereal, almost.

Benes waited nervously at the front, heads turned, friends smiled as they walked slowly past. It was reassuring. Irena hadn't been to church since her father had died, and she looked choked by what Jana imagined were difficult memories. It was a building which now held snapshots of their family life. It was a day her sister was meant to enjoy, but it was also tinged with loss.

Jana watched Irena grip Aleš's arm so tightly that it looked as though she was afraid of what would happen if she let go. Her frail body might not hold up to the pressure of standing alone – her body, and maybe her emotions. Jana knew the heartache she was fighting.

Benes beamed in her direction as the party arrived at the front of the church. The service was short but emotional, tissues were pulled out of bags and heads were bowed. Some looked deep in thought, others glanced at loved ones.

The celebrations later were full of laughter and fun. Irena tolerated the obligatory bridal kidnapping with her usual grace for un-planned events. Friends held her hostage at a bar in Prague, and those who stayed behind gathered money for her release.

The screams of laughter brought more revellers into the

bar. Jana watched well-wishers buy them drinks and admire her sister's dress. She was so glad to see Irena happy.

Meanwhile, the men were on a bar crawl through town to search for the missing bride – the groom having to buy drinks until Irena was found. Feeling responsible for the bride, Jana announced that there was now enough money to take her back to the wedding party. A friend had arrived minutes earlier with all the coins, and Lida went to find the groom to tell him where his wife could be found.

They returned to the reception and the dancing continued. When it came to the *kolibka,* Jana held up a plate as the guests threw coins on to it. The money was, as is tradition, for Irena, her husband and their future children. Guests threw in generous amounts of coins and banknotes. Jana counted out the koruna later and kept them safely.

The dancing went on into the night. Jana laughed as she saw her mother dancing with her uncle. He swung her around the room, just missing some of the other guests. It reminded her of watching her parents dance. Matka looked relaxed and happy. She had been determined to immerse herself in the events of the day. Jana's uncle danced with their neighbour, Alicia. Jana hadn't imagined what it would be like to watch all these people dance.

It was a hilarious mix of Polka and Cossack dancing. The men at the front of the room playing the fiddle were now moving through the crowd. One man played the balalaika, which Jana recognised from the triangular shape. Her brother had tried to play it when he was younger.

Children ran around wildly, weaving in and out of the movement. Jana wanted to join them but she knew she was neither small enough nor fast enough to keep up, and she was meant to behave like an adult. She had so wanted to dance with Tatínek, but Aleš scooped her up off her chair and they joined in with whatever was playing at the time. He was a much better dancer and he twirled her around effortlessly. She felt safe following his lead. For the most part Jana felt as though she was on the outside looking in. It was a feeling to which she had become accustomed.

As the music faded, people started to put chairs out in a large circle, and women were brought forward by the men to sit on the chairs. Lida tied a scarf over Benes' eyes and spun him round. He proceeded to get down onto the floor and feel the knees of all the ladies in the room. This tradition had baffled Jana – not that she had been to many weddings – but she wondered how the groom was meant to guess which one was his wife and what would happen to their honeymoon if he made a wrong judgement. Was he meant to just take another woman? How would he know which one was her sister?

All her relatives were now laughing and clapping as if they were about to witness a bullfight. Irena looked nervous. Jana couldn't blame her and didn't envy her sister, or her new husband, for the humiliation they were about to undergo. Beyond the room, and the bustle of the wedding party, the city lights illuminated the spires of the cathedral. The tables were covered in flower petals and decorations, and the place looked full of life and celebration. It reminded her of Christmas, but it was now hot and humid. The evening light was stunning with the rich colours in the backdrop of the sky, and in those moments everything was perfect.

Looking through the crowd, which was now gathering at quite a pace, Jana could see Benes on his knees pretending not to enjoy the task of stroking all the female legs in the party in order to find and claim his wife. Women giggled and teased him, and the men clapped and made jokes about his lack of navigational skills.

Children held down the scarf to stop him cheating and, when he finally found his wife, there was laughter and more toasting. A considerable amount of alcohol was being consumed and Jana wondered if she needed some more to help her enter into the frivolities. She felt her sisterly duties were done, and needed something to help her relax.

Jana found a vodka cocktail at the bar and drank it quickly. The fire in her throat was intense, reminding her all the more of celebrations with Miloš's family, and of Miloš. Letovice was now a distant memory but thoughts of him still lingered. She wanted him to be with her right here, with all her family and friends. It felt strange without him. He would have danced, and he wouldn't have let her sit down all evening. She liked the feeling of the heat from the vodka and went in search of another.

The bride and groom were now witnesses to the plate smashing taking place in front of them, followed by someone handing them a brush to clear it up. This was meant to show how they would co-operate and work together through married life. Jana wondered how that would work in principle and what it might be like to share her life with someone. It was an alien concept, and one that brought all sorts of trouble from what she had seen in different relationships. Her parents had been an exception but it was strange that you were suddenly meant to share everything, especially when most of life taught you to be resolutely independent.

Her thoughts were broken by the sound of laughter from the other side of the room. Some of her family were looking at some old baby photographs of Irena. As Jana walked over she saw Matka pointing to the photograph of her and Irena dressed up as soldiers for a school play. Her uncles and aunts laughed at the stern look on Jana's face in the photograph. It was her normal face, her thoughtful face. How could they laugh?

The days that followed the wedding provided time to talk to Aleš and Matka. She had missed time spent with them walking around the city and evenings spent with friends. Jana wrote to Miloš each week and they spoke on the phone from time to time. Life in Letovice remained the same and she would always ask about Babička.

Being in Prague felt strangely freeing. She missed people in Letovice but it was important for her to be here now. Her sister had needed her support before the wedding and she was able to share the work with Aleš and help to sort family finances and paperwork for Matka.

It had been good to see old friends and to go to some of the places that she had visited with Tatínek. It had helped her to come to terms with the reality that he was no longer alive. Loss was an inexplicable experience, leaving the bearer with a strange sense of emptiness, without being able to place a finger on the exact details. It made all other parts of life lose their lustre.

Jana felt demotivated and, at times, powerless. These were feelings she learned to push through. The truth of it was that each day did get easier. Having to endure loss made it easier to understand others. She was seeing things in a different light, and the pain didn't actually break her in the way that she had feared. There was hope for whatever lay ahead, and Jana was grateful for the time she had spent with Tatínek before he had gone. The word, 'gone,' sounded so final.

She spent afternoons reminiscing with Matka and Aleš. They talked of family holidays and the wild ideas Tatínek had had when he was about to write a paper or give a key lecture. He would practise his theories on them and expect a succinct critique and a careful breakdown of his words.

They had learned to humour him, and he had relied on Jana for most of the feedback. Although her knowledge of economics was slim, she had a sharp, agile mind.

Matka would often scurry off to make tea, while Aleš would play with a pencil and pretend to be listening when he was often miles away. He was a great talker, but not when his father was ranting about his work. Aleš would shut down and slip into his own world.

Jana couldn't deny that she wanted to soak up all there was to know about life, about the economic workings of the State, especially when Tatínek discussed politics. She loved the subject with the same passion, and her eyes would light up when he talked about revolution. This only encouraged him to go further into the debate, and she would lean on one arm like a cat lying in the sun with its head on one paw. She was at home in the city but her thoughts were always with Miloš.

Chapter 9

The sun pierced through the gaps in between the buildings, its rays caught the edges of the gables, shimmering against the window panes. It was August – the summer was in full swing. Jana had met with friends for coffee and a pastry earlier and wanted to visit a museum to make the most of her time in the city before leaving for Letovice. The Jewish Museum, being at the top of her list, she hoped would provide the opportunity to learn more about the Jewish settlement in Prague, and the effects of the Holocaust. Horrific stories had been told about the persecution of Jews but she knew very little of their history. There were many places still to visit, despite the fact that she had grown up in the city. For some reason this would be an important place to visit, on this particular day. Jana wandered across the bridge towards the old town, feeling the heat of the sun on her face. The warmth was welcome.

The skies were crystal clear and the views of the city across the river were unlike any other skyline she could imagine. She weaved her way downhill through the old buildings, never really having observed the varying outlines of the buildings on Nerudova Street, where she found herself gazing at the symbols embellishing the buildings. There were many characteristic signs and statues built into the facades of the houses. Some had primarily belonged to Czech violin-makers or goldsmiths. Others belonged to writers and art historians. Each told a story of a city steeped in history. There were stories to be told from small symbols, many of which were still largely intact, but often unnoticed.

The house at Nerudova Street 34, the Golden Horseshoe, had belonged to the Italian builder Avostalis. The picture of St Wenceslas boasted a real horseshoe on the foot of the horse. These works of art had been an indication of the profession of the owner, before buildings were numbered. Tatínek had once told her that the oldest known house signs found their origins in third century Egypt, where house signs told people that the occupant was able to interpret dreams. She had dreamed that night as a young girl of a house with a dove on the facade, she dreamed that freedom would let her fly.

Gothic spires and baroque domes ruled the skyline. They spoke of rulers, princes, emperors and kingdoms. Jana wondered if other cities were as beautiful as this, or if it was her familiarity with the place that made it her own private idyl. As she reached Staroměstské náměstí, the Old Town Square, she could see the astronomical clock of the Old Town Hall.

The golden hands and Roman numerals on the clock face glistened in the light, announcing the time. The inner circle slowly traced the movement of the sun and moon around the earth. It was nearly midday. She stood and waited, others gathered round and, as the hand struck twelve exactly, the twelve apostles travelled across the windows above the circles. This hourly event reminded Jana of her brother's musical box. Jana's grandmother had given it to Matka as a child and when they opened the lid the soldier would turn around slowly. He reminded her of the castle guards, but smaller and less threatening.

The colours of the Old Town Square were vibrant in the late morning light, and the buildings breathtakingly beautiful in all four seasons. She savoured scenes of Prague in the snow – it was a magical place when the red rooftops turned to pure white like a scene from a picture book – unrealistic, almost.

Wandering further along Pařížská Street into Josefov, she reached one of the smallest quarters of the City. The Jewish quarter was full of synagogues and unusual buildings, with two clocks visible on the front of the Jewish town hall building. The upper clock face had Roman numerals and the lower clock face revealed Hebrew writing. It demanded the viewer's attention with its golden symbols on a dark face. The hands rotated anticlockwise to follow the numerals. Both clocks reached half past twelve. The same time, reached from entirely different directions. Didn't people often reach the same points in life from different directions?

The diversity of the designs and the cultures, living parallel lives in the same space, reminded Jana of words Tatínek used to say, ideas about people's differences. He detested the uniformity of it all – the systems and the structures. If he were here now he would be talking, reasoning, explaining. She enjoyed the silence.

Jana wandered into the Maisel Synagogue, now a museum, it displayed a range of ceremonial silver, artifacts that were unfamiliar, paintings and books. She read the detail below each item and discovered that the Jewish community had settled here in the twelfth century. There had been a Talmudic school and a Hebrew printing press. Emperor Joseph II had relaxed many of the restrictions on the 'ghetto' which had formed, and in 1849 Josefov became part of the city.

This was so much more interesting than reading history books or listening to teachers, to actually see places, to go into buildings and learn from real places. History at school had always been two-dimensional with the over-learning of facts and figures, the memorising of numbers and dates that made no sense. Even when Tatínek spoke about history and politics, it still wasn't the same as watching the dismantling of the wall on their television screen, or marching in the crowds on that day, with their flags, feeling the atmosphere rising.

Tombstones filled the nearby Jewish cemetery. The graveyard looked like a collapsed building with peaks of stone. Not one stood upright. They reflected a mournfulness and neglect, possibly from the resulting chaos of squeezing in 12,000 tombs. Jana looked again at her book. She had deliberated over taking it from Tatínek's shelf earlier that morning. Yes, 12,000, how did they all fit in? She was even more shocked to discover that beneath them lay more than 100,000 bodies.

It was hard to imagine what these people's lives had been like and what had happened to them prior to their premature deaths. Why had this group of people had to suffer so much persecution? She became painfully aware of her own ignorance. She knew little about Hitler but understood the insanity of attempting to wipe out an entire race. The Jews, from what little information she had gleaned, were an intelligent group of people. Blessed by God, some would say.

How could human nature be so vile? Would this happen again, further on in history, to different people groups and nations? Was this the beginning of further brutality? Where had it begun? Jana was fearful that an end to the communist regime might give rise to too much freedom and leave people open to the perils of some other individual or regime – one that would sweep in and change the world around them with new and dangerous ideologies.

Her thoughts began to frighten her but were quickly interrupted by the sight of a bird landing on one of the larger tombstones. She looked more closely. The tomb had the inscription of Mordechai Maisel, and the date 1602. Some of the tombstones were made of stone and had simple inscriptions like this one. Others were marble and had elaboate decoration. She could see from the dates that were still legible that these were the later burials. Some had symbols carefully carved into them, showing the trade of the individual.

Turning to face the Ceremonial Hall looming over the right-hand side of the cemetery, the Chevra Kadisha Building, Jana noticed the turrets, like a miniature castle. This was the museum that Tatínek had promised to take her to but their trip had never materialised. She thought about what he might have said to her but was glad to be alone and to make up her own mind. Jana took a breath and walked up the steep stone steps under the archway.

The building was dark and narrow. Inside, it was filled with children's drawings and poems from Terezin, the concentration camp that had been situated to the north-east of Prague. Jana, and a few other visitors, witnessed the devastating depictions of the camps through children's drawings. They had been crammed into simple wood bunk beds from the appearance of many of the drawings. There were pictures of children crying. It was chilling.

Jana caught sight of a picture of a pile of children's shoes. She saw a man standing further back with tears rolling down his cheeks. He was looking at the same picture. Jana looked closely at him and realised that she recognised his face. She decided to walk on, at least until she had worked out how she knew him.

In the next room she remembered that he had come to the apartment a week before the wedding and given her a present for Irena. His name escaped her but she remembered what she had liked about him.

She turned back. He was gone. The rest of the museum was just as alarming in its representation of the Holocaust. The images and the words were both vivid and heart-rending. Some of the children had been extremely young. At the same time, Jana couldn't get rid of the image in her mind of the man with the tears rolling down his cheeks.

Trying to absorb the images was challenging. Looking at the pictures put the viewer in touch with the brutal reality of it in a way that a photograph or a book would fail to achieve. These innocent drawings were so much more personal and powerful, snapping the viewer into the frame of events with sharp focus.

As she made her way to the stairs at the top of the building, Jana caught sight of the man. He looked vulnerable and he was obviously shaken by the exhibits in the museum. Jana wanted to talk to him, but was afraid that he wouldn't remember her. What if he wanted to just be alone? It wasn't respectful timing. She had nothing to lose, except her dignity, and she may not see him again. She wanted to take the initiative, take a risk and hope.

'I'm sorry to disturb you, my name is Jana. I'm Irena's sister.'

He looked confused, as if he didn't understand the language she was using. Maybe he didn't speak Czech. She tried speaking to him in English and he smiled.

'Ah, yes, I remember.' He responded in Czech. 'I was somewhere else. You were at the house when I dropped by.'

His response sounded so vague, almost as if he didn't care. He did speak her native language, as she now remembered.

'You're Czech?'

'Yes, of course. Why do you ask?'

'Sorry, it's none of my business.' Jana hesitated. She felt foolish asking him where he was from when she didn't even know him. He wiped his eyes, which were still damp, and held his hand out towards hers.

'That's OK. Let's start again, I'm Lukas.'

She remembered he was a friend of Benes.

'Yes, I remember.'

'You've caught me at a bad time. I found this more upsetting than I expected.'

'I know what you mean, it's disturbing but important,' she said philosophically.

'Yes, it's ironic that all these things have been preserved because of Hitler.'

'Really? How?'

'He ordered many of the synagogue artefacts to be confiscated from Bohemia and Moravia. Items were taken from all over the Czech Republic.' Jana couldn't get used to the new name, it felt unfamiliar and strange, like an unwelcome guest. 'You see, he wanted to set up a museum here in Josefov for what he believed would be an extinct race. By some divine grace, or something like it, these people were saved. There are still at least a thousand Jews living in this quarter today.'

'How do you know all of this?'

'I've just read a lot, and my mother has always talked to me about it. I think she wanted me to know about my heritage, and to understand some of the persecution that my ancestors endured. Some survived and some didn't. I wouldn't be here today if Hitler's plans had prevailed.'

Jana was impressed by his honesty and his knowledge but his obvious distress made her uncomfortable.

'What's amazing,' he continued, 'is that the very things he preserved for his purposes have been used today as a memorial for those who died, and a reminder that many survived the atrocities. Those artefacts are now exhibited in three of the restored synagogues.'

'I went into one of them this morning,' she said. 'It was beautiful.'

'Shall we go outside? This isn't the best place to talk.'

Jana followed him out into the street and stood looking at the cemetery. It sat serenely in the dappled light filtering through the trees.

'Why wasn't this demolished?' asked Jana.

'Soldiers were ordered to destroy Jewish cemeteries but this one was preserved for the museum. It's the oldest existing one in Europe, and has been here since 1439.'

'I know it's a strange thing to say, but it's beautiful.'

'Isn't it?'

'Do you have any family here? You mentioned your heritage – you're Jewish?' she glaced at the gravestones.

'Yes. My mother's family name was Morawitz. Her brother died in one of the camps but she doesn't talk about him much. I think it's too painful. Apparently she was with him when he died. Many became ill, they were crammed into such a small space. I think they lost him quite quickly.'

'I'm so sorry.'

'He was older than her and there were only the two of them. They were separated from their parents.'

'That must have been awful.' Her words didn't feel adequate but she felt compelled to continue. 'I can't begin to imagine what it must have been like. Under those conditions you'd never know if you would see anyone again.'

'My mother only spoke about the history in general terms. I think it must have been hard for her to talk about her personal experiences. She probably blocked much of it from her memory. She was reunited with her parents but the scars never really leave you. No one can take away the memory of what happened. I used to cry as a boy when she talked about it so she would stop. I often wonder whether she would have told me more if I'd been able to bear it.'

'I don't know what to say. It's so personal for you and I'm an onlooker, an ignorant one.'

She felt his sadness and his tears in the museum made sense. Lukas smiled and looked down at his shoes. She watched him tuck his hands deep into the pockets of his trousers. They both stood in silence. It was more comforting than it was awkward. She was intrigued by what he had shared and felt at ease in his company. Drawn in by his vulnerability, she wanted to understand.

'I was thinking of getting some lunch,' she said. 'Do you want to join me? Only if you want to, no pressure. I'm going anyway and I just thought…'

'Yes.' He stopped her in her tracks. 'That would be good.'

'There's a café nearby that serves lunch.'

'Great.'

They wandered for a while through the streets asking each other questions and talking openly. It was as if they had known each other for more than a few moments. They reached the café and found a table by the window. Jana sat facing the street.

'What were you saying earlier,' asked Lukas, 'about being away from your parents? When did that happen?'

'I spent six months in Letovice.'

'Where's that?'

'It's a town near Boskovice, just North of Brno.'

'Doing what, exactly?'

'Physical therapy. I work in a school for disabled children, just trying to help them through different exercises, strengthen their muscles.'

'When are you going back?'

'End of the summer.'

She wanted to stay here, where she felt at home. It made her feel closer to Tatínek. She wanted everything to stand still, unchanged.

'What's it like?' Lukas asked.

'It's interesting. There are some wonderful people. I stayed with a family for a while.' Jana didn't want to go into detail, she tried to avoid the subject of Miloš.

'Tell me more.'

She was surprised that he was interested, especially after the heavy conversation they had had about his family history and the museum.

'I came back for my sister's wedding and I've spent the rest of the summer catching up with friends and spending time with my family.'

His hand cupped the coffee mug. He drank from it slowly, watching her as she stumbled over her words. Most of them, refusing to roll off her tongue with any ease or grace.

'There are people in Letovice who I miss deeply, but Prague is my home. It was an open-ended job and I said I would go for six months initially. The conversation about how long hasn't come up for a while, and I've tried to ignore it.'

'It sounds as though there are people who would value your return, but I can understand.'

She felt selfish for wanting to stay. She needed to see Miloš. It was difficult to think clearly after this morning. There had been much to take in and she didn't want to talk about herself. It made her feel uncomfortable.

'Thank you, we'll see. What about you? What do you do?'

'I'm a conservator. I work for the Institute of Archeology here in the city.'

'I'm not sure I know it.'

'It joined the Academy of Science this year. I work mainly on the protection of ancient and historical monuments.'

'It sounds interesting.'

'I enjoy the work, but the bureaucracy of it can be complicated. You have to know how the system works.'

'You sound like my father. To him life was full of systems.'

'What does he do?'

'Did. He died two years ago.' It was easier to say this time around.

'Benes did tell me, but I hadn't put two and two together. I'm sorry, really clumsy of me.'

'It's OK, really.'

'What happened, if you don't mind me asking?'

'He became ill and he never really recovered. His lungs were weak.' Jana didn't feel like going into detail. 'Tell me more about your job.'

'What do you want to know?'

'Anything, what's it like? What have you worked on?'

He smiled and looked into her eyes. 'I'm sure your job is more worthwhile. You're helping people, I'm just protecting historical objects and buildings.'

'That's important too. We need history, and we need evidence of it.'

Their plates were taken away and Jana started to play nervously with her napkin. Lukas had a disarming style. Jana liked the way he didn't take the trivial things in life too deeply. He was a thinker and she felt happy discussing things that were important with him. She felt that he wouldn't judge or criticise her the way she had first expected.

Chapter 10

This was the letter Miloš had been waiting for. He was almost at the end of his studies and he was keen to get some fieldwork experience. There was so much more he could do abroad than at home in Letovice. Besides, he knew there would be many people applying to work at the Boskovice hospital, or in Brno. He wanted to work with those who had been marginalised, but he didn't have the money to help them, just an able body and a willingness to learn.

Dear Mr Martinek,

Thank you for your offer of help with our medical care. The Daylight Project has been working with the Badjao community in Davao for five years with continued support from sponsors from as far afield as New Zealand, Canada and Russia. We believe that healthcare is of primary concern to this particular group of people, and would value your skills on our team. The team is comprised of professionals and volunteers. You will find that there is much to learn both from the team and from these indigenous people. If you have any further questions regarding our work in the Philippines please contact us.

Please let us know when you could start and for how long you will be available. We also need two references before we can consider your application.

Yours sincerely,

R. Wade
(Director, Daylight Project)

Miloš held the letter tightly and reread it. He wanted to take all the details and mull over the offer. He had written to them, along with other charities and hospitals in different parts of the world, after Jana left, in the hope that someone would take him. Despite the fact that he wasn't yet qualified, he wanted the chance to be useful. He had almost forgotten that he had written to them when the letter arrived. Only a few years ago it would have been almost an impossibility to get there. Travel restrictions had now been lifted.

Knowing few facts about the Philippines made it an intriguing place to travel to, and their response sounded positive. He was excited about the opportunity and it would take his mind away from the constant thoughts of Jana. Miloš wasn't sure how she would feel but he knew she wouldn't try to stop him. She had left and they both needed to carry on with their lives. The distance shouldn't change anything between them. That is what he told himself until the day that he stepped on to a plane bound for Manila.

The Martinek family were missing Jana over the summer and they all continually asked Miloš questions about how she was, and passed on their love. Sometimes she spoke to them when she rang, but often he would answer in the hope that he would hear her voice. Miloš knew Jana was likely to ring on Sunday afternoons but on other occasions Kamila would reach the phone first, and when she heard the familiar voice on the other end of the line they would chat about whatever girls talked about.

He never knew what they found to talk about for so long. Girls had a strange way of being able to talk about anything and nothing. He was becoming more nervous of talking to her as time went by. The occasions when Kamila intercepted the calls were a moment for him to gather his thoughts. She didn't have the same need to impress Jana.

He worried that they were drifting apart. What if Jana was enjoying Prague too much to return? Some of the memories were fading and he clung on to the details – the image of her red dress, conversations about books, watching her drink the fire juice. Trying to hang on to memories is like trying to reach your shadow. The more you reach out, the further away it appears to move. Miloš disliked the physical and emotional distance, and he wasn't keen on phone conversations. You can never read someone's facial expressions or body language. He didn't believe that you could communicate honestly from a distance and he longed to see her, to hold her and to talk about the summer, the letter, the offer.

'What's that you're reading?' said Mrs Martinek as she walked into the kitchen.

'It's a letter from a charity offering some voluntary work abroad.'

Mrs Martinek put down the pile of sheets and sat at the table.

'What sort of work? Who are they?'

Miloš saw the look in her eyes, she looked troubled. 'It's from a charity called Daylight. They want me to help them with some medical care in the Philippines. I'd love to go. What do you think?' He looked up at her.

'Well, you're young. You need to make the most of every opportunity now that you have the chance to travel. We didn't.' Her voice trailed off.

'I know. Will you be alright?'

'Of course, go. Enjoy the chance to see the world. It's your decision. No one can make it for you. Don't feel torn. I know you haven't exactly been yourself since she left but you have to do what's important and it sounds like a good opportunity.

Miloš sloped out of the room and left the house to get some fresh air. He regretted having told his mother about Jana. Maybe things would have been easier if he hadn't. The air was getting colder and the leaves were starting to turn. It didn't feel the same walking through Letovice without her. He found himself outside the restaurant that he had taken her to before she left. He thought of that night, and remembered the lost look in her eyes when she talked about her father. How was she now? It must have been so hard for her to go home. She hadn't really talked about it.

He stared through the window and he must have been there for a while. His friend Tomas came out to see if he was all right. He managed to persuade Miloš to come in for a coffee. Tomas was off duty for a while so they sat together and talked, mainly about mundane things.

'Where is she? The one you brought here that night?'

'Jana? She's in Prague.'

'Didn't manage to hang on to her, then?' he asked, slapping Miloš on the back playfully.

'She had a family wedding. She's coming back and she's not mine.'

'Shame. Interesting, isn't she?'

'Yes, I suppose she is.' He wondered what it was about Jana that was so intriguing to someone who had only just met her. It was hard to put a finger on what it was about her. She had a quality that made people sit up and take notice. Maybe it was the way she looked at you or listened, maybe it was her directness at times, or her insight. He didn't know, but he knew he liked her, he admired her. Miloš put the cup down and stood up.

'Thanks for the coffee, I'd better get going.'

He wanted to avoid any further conversation about Jana. He

was flattered that his friend liked her, and glad that she was his. Miloš wondered whether or not it was good when your friends liked your girlfriend. The line between approval and a possible threat to the relationship was not always clearly drawn. They shook hands and he left. It wasn't as cold today as it had been on the day that they went for a walk. It was lonely.

As he stood watching the burnt amber leaves spiraling to the ground he wondered what the future would hold for him and for them. He decided that he would go to the Philippines. Time couldn't stand still and the summer had been long enough. His restlessness and need for a new challenge was increasing by the day. He couldn't just wait for her return, he had to keep busy and make the most of his time. This was an opportunity he'd been dreaming of for years, so what was it that was holding him back? Fear, maybe.

Chapter 11

Jana closed the letter from Miloš and glanced out of the window. The street was empty. There was an absence of the usual morning hustle and bustle. The place felt strangely quiet. Catching her breath, she wondered why Miloš hadn't said he was leaving Letovice. She was supposed to be returning soon. Didn't he want to see her? Maybe he had found the distance too difficult, or maybe he was tired of waiting. The Philippines would be an exciting venture for him.

She could feel the ever-increasing void between them. The summer had been spent soaking up the addictive atmosphere of the city, breathing in memories of the past. Irena's wedding had come and gone, memories of her father had lost their sharpness.

A knock at the door interrupted her thoughts. She placed the letter carefully into a drawer under the cutlery and dropped her coffee mug into the sink. Opening the front door slowly, Jana saw a familiar face.

'Morning,' said Lukas. 'I hope it's not too presumptuous but I wondered if we could go for a coffee, or a walk?' He put his hand in his pockets and curled his lower lip. 'Don't worry if you're busy, that's fine. I can come back another time. I can see that now is not so good.'

'No, no,' said Jana, 'now is fine. Coffee would be great, I mean it's no problem.' His smile was irresistible. 'I'll get my jacket, there's a place I know and I could do with the company.'

'Are you OK?'

'Yes, fine, I was miles away, that's all. Nothing really. I just...' Her voice faded as she disappeared into the kitchen. Lukas stood at the doorstep and Jana reappeared with her bag. 'Don't mind me. How are you? Where have you been?'

'Working. I enjoyed our lunch the other day, so I thought I'd come and find you.'

'And you remembered where I live.'

'Of course.'

Jana wanted to sit on her feelings – feelings that the letter had unearthed – and Lukas was a welcome distraction.

They strolled along her street, talking about archaeology, Prague, Letovice, families, and politics. Their conversation became heated at times and would remind her of conversations she had had with Tatínek. In some curious way there were similarities between the two. It was strange, the way she felt the familiarity of his company even though she hadn't known him for long. They walked towards the river and talked about Irena and Benes. Jana held her head up to feel the wind on her face.

'How's it going?' he asked.

'Hmm?'

'Being home. How is it?'

'Good. It's been a great summer and tt feels as though I've never been away. I love this city, it's stunning, don't you think?'

'I wouldn't go that far.'

'It is. Where else would you find a castle and a cathedral like this? And what about the bridges, the river, the buildings, the beer?'

'You sound like a tour guide, or a student.'

'Don't be ridiculous. You know what I mean, Charles Bridge is unique. Well, I like it.'

'OK.'

'What do you mean, OK?'

'I mean you're entitled to your opinion. I like it, but I've been here for too long.'

'Well, it's home to me and there's nowhere like it.'

'Aren't you leaving soon?'

'Lukas, can we talk about something else?'

The small café was busy and their conversation was lost in the bustle and noise. Jana kept thinking about the letter and it made her feel lost. It was unusual for her to feel like this in her own city. She remembered feeling similarly lost in Letovice from time to time, but not here.

Looking up at Lukas, she watched his mop of dark curls fall across his face as he sipped his coffee.

'So what are you working on?' she asked.

'We're trying to sort through and identify some Renaissance tiles at the castle. There were some excavations which finished a few years ago and we have the task of sifting through the glass from the digs to identify their origins.'

'It sounds interesting.'

'It helps us to study the way glass was used in everyday life. Some of it is baroque glass so it's a lot of work for the teams involved.'

'You enjoy what you're doing, though?'

'You have to. It's hours and hours of work and the process can be very slow and frustrating. I'm also working on a bigger project. We're restoring a mosaic at the castle.

'Sounds interesting.'

'There is a lot of groundwork to be done before we begin. It'll be years of work.'

'It's good that they've asked you to be on the team.'

'Yes, although I can't say that I'm the most experienced. The advisory group is made up of historians, conservators and archaeologists. Some are more experienced than me.'

'I'm sure you know what you're doing.'

She had remembered her father saying things that were worth doing were worth taking time over. 'So your free time is in short supply.'

He smiled. 'I think we can manage a few coffees. I'll pay and we can walk along the river, your river.'

She blushed. 'It's not mine.'

'In your city,' he added.

She pulled her jacket over her shoulder and clutched it, as if hoping it would shield her. Lukas opened the door and they wandered out into the street. Walking in silence for a while, they enjoyed the peace. It was a rare thing to be in the company of someone and not need to talk. She liked his company for the very reason that the silences were as comfortable as the conversation. He kicked the leaves across the grass and threw sticks into the distance.

They sat on the bench in Stromovka Park by the fountain and he threw stones into the water. She watched the ripples. He reminded her of a boy at school. Lukas was considerably older but it was difficult to tell how much older than her. Jana looked across at him and stroked the back of his neck. He turned and looked at her but before he could say anything, she kissed him.

He pulled back, looking confused. Jana looked away and stared into the fountain, as if it hadn't happened, watching the water gushing out and falling gracefully into the pool below. She felt strangely liberated, despite his reaction. She had wanted to do that, to do something, for a while.

This morning's letter was perhaps the trigger. It clarified the rolling thoughts of Miloš and made a way through the confusion, the longing to seize this moment.

'What was that for?' Lukas had tried to hold her gaze. Her mind was a jumble of excitement, guilt and – seconds later – shock.

'I just felt like it,' she said boldly, pulling her shoulders back.

'I thought you were...'

'Seeing someone?' she finished his sentence.

'Yes, I mean... I didn't think you were interested in me. Not like that, and what about the boy?'

'Miloš?' said Jana defiantly.

'Isn't he waiting for you?'

'How do you know about him?' she demanded.

'Benes told me, I think your sister told him.'

'If you call leaving the country for the Philippines waiting for someone then yes, I suppose so.'

'Hold on. Have I missed something?'

'No, I don't think so.' She swept her hair back behind one ear. Tired of resisting change and waiting for everything in life to just happen, a new boldness had taken hold of her. She was tired of being fearful and cautious. No, this was how it should be.

'Well, explain.'

'I just kissed you.'

'Yes, I noticed. You know what I mean. What's going on? I thought this was all out of bounds. I really like you, but I didn't think anything could happen...'

Before he could finish the sentence she kissed him again. Lukas pulled her away gently and looked at her. He looked startled.

'OK. Talk,' he said.

'I don't want to talk. I've had enough of thinking and

talking. Lukas, my father took decisions and just moved forwards. He changed things. He actively followed his beliefs. I don't want to waste my life worrying. Meeting you has given me a new perspective on things.'

'Yes, I can see that.'

'I've realised that you can't resist change. Things move on, whether you like it or not. You have to figure out where you are going. You have to make a decision and run with it, even if there is a risk that it might be a wrong one. It's inertia and passivity that crushes your soul, it eats away at your mind and paralyses you.'

'Jana, what's going on?'

'I can't see it working with Miloš' she said, 'not while we're in different places.' She hesitated before finishing the sentence. 'I just haven't told him, but it's not working.'

'What do you want, Jana?'

'I like you,' she said. 'I really like you. Maybe I wasn't being honest with you or myself. I don't know, but I know how I feel when I'm with you. You make me feel alive. You make me think and see things more clearly. It's as if there's some kind of link between us.'

'We haven't known each other for that long, Jana, and you don't know much about me.'

'I know,' she said quietly.

Lukas looked uneasy. 'You seem so strangely familiar. You're beautiful and intelligent, Jana, but something doesn't seem right. I feel bad about the boy but there's something else. I can't work out what it is, but I can't do this. I'm sorry. I didn't think we'd be in this situation.'

'What do you mean?'

'Well, I just thought we were friends.'

Jana stared directly at him. 'OK. Let's be just that,' she said. 'Forget any of this and we'll go back to how things were.'

Her words sounded resolute as she spoke but she felt crushed. She couldn't seem to convey the right message. She had been coy and reserved with Miloš and it made her want to run in the opposite direction with Lukas. Something inside her wanted to break out. The situation looked as though it now needed to be reversed. She had gone too far.

'No,' said Lukas, 'I mean, I don't want to just stop. I want to be clear in my mind about what's happening.'

'I see.'

'No you don't. I think you're great, but I just wasn't expecting it. You took me by surprise.'

'Do you plan everything?'

She knew she wasn't helping herself but her frustration was steadily rising. He got up and walked towards the fountain, picked up a handful of stones from the ground and started to skim them across the surface of the water. Each one travelled further towards the other side.

Jana got up from the bench and walked over to the water. She stood next to Lukas, not wanting to look at him for fear of seeing a look of disapproval.

'I didn't mean it like that,' she said, breaking the silence. 'I just didn't think it would be that much of a surprise to you.'

'Are you doing this to punish someone?'

'What do you mean?' How could he think like that?

'I mean exactly that. You seem frustrated. I can't help thinking I'm your way out of whatever it is you are running from. I really want to be with you, but not for the wrong reasons, Jana.'

She turned and walked away, unable to face the questions. The reality was that she felt mad with Tatínek for having left them all. It wasn't his fault, she knew that, yet she blamed him. Why hadn't Miloš waited for her? He was doing the best thing for his life and it didn't have to revolve around her but she wanted him to need her. How could she explain it to Lukas? It wasn't any of his business. She had managed to hold everything together for this long. It wasn't so terrible that she liked him. Jana had made a bold move, one that would be difficult to go back on.

She weaved her way through the trees and out of the park, leaving Lukas sitting on the edge of the fountain. She tried not to look back, walking faster with each pace. Why had he talked about running? Tatínek used to say the same thing. There were a lot of similar phrases that she had heard them both using. Lukas had a sharp edge to him and he was strangely similar to Tatínek in his outlook.

Chapter 12

Sitting on the train heading for Prague, Miloš felt a deep, sinking feeling in the pit of his stomach, reminding him of school days. Like taking an exam, you never knew whether you would succeed or barely scrape through. The imminent meeting with Jana in Prague felt similar.

He wondered if she really did want to see him before he flew to Manila. She'd called him when the letter arrived, but he couldn't help thinking that it was just to see how she felt about him. It was cynical – he knew that – but the distance had taken its toll on them both and things had changed since she left Letovice.

He thought of Jana walking into their living room in the red dress. The way she teased him brought a smile to his lips momentarily. They had been playful then but the distance had brought a serious tone to their relationship that was, at times, suffocating.

The journey felt endless and he wondered what they would talk about. Would she still be the same? He wanted to hold her and to see her face, but there was a fear that accompanied the longing and it was set to stay with him until they met.

As the train drew into the station he caught sight of her at the end of the platform. Looking nervous, Jana waved and walked towards his carriage. His mouth felt dry and his pulse quickened. Miloš hauled his suitcase off the rack, opened the door, and stepped off the train.

They walked tentatively towards each other and he dropped his case as he reached her, grasping her hands. They were clammy.

'Let me look at you. I've been trying to remember the details of your face.'

Jana giggled nervously as he grabbed her and hugged her. He released her and stepped back.

'Well? Aren't you going to say anything?'

She shook her head. 'I can't, I mean I don't know what to say.'

'All this time, and you don't know what to say? What's happened to you, Jana? You never used to be lost for words.'

'It's so good to see you,' she said.

'Is it?'

'Of course. It's been ages.'

'You just don't look … pleased.'

'I'm just nervous, that's all.' Her head rolled to one side.

'Nervous of what?' He wanted to sound confident.

'Miloš, we haven't seen each other all summer.'

He felt a glass wall between them lift, now that he could see her face. As they walked towards the exit and onto the street, he slipped his hand into hers. She glanced at him a few times with a look that he couldn't read. He hoped she would know better than to ask a guy what he was thinking. He willed her not to ask too many questions,

'I wonder,' said Miloš, 'if by the time I come home you might be back in Letovice.' He smiled.

'I don't know,' she put a finger up to her mouth, 'I have to think. I'm not sure if I can stand more Becherovka.'

'Don't drink it like that, girl.' He mimicked his father's voice. 'Take it all in one go. It's the best, all the way from Karlovy Vary.'

She giggled. 'My throat is still recovering.'

'Jana, you have to come back. Work needs you. Babička needs you. She misses you.'

'Really? They need me?' She sounded unsure of herself. Her voice reminded him of the way she was when she told him about her father.

'I don't know, Miloš. There are places here where I can do my work too.'

'I can't tell you what to do any more than you can direct my life,' he said.

'I suppose not. I just need time to work out what to do next. I don't want to get trapped into something that's not right.'

'I know what you mean,' he said. 'I want to go travelling, I want to see life before it takes hold of me and makes its demands.'

'I need to know if there's a future for us, Miloš. I'm not sure where I fit into your carefree existence at the moment.'

'Carefree?' He scrunched his face.

'Well, you seem to be using your trip to the Philippines as an excuse to run from things, from me, maybe.'

'Jana, there are people in the community I'm going to visit who need help and I want to, in some small way, make a difference to their lives.'

'That's very heroic.' She sounded more feisty than she had been in Letovice, almost angry.

'I'm sorry, Miloš. Ignore me. I'm just frustrated about being so far away from you, and I miss Tatínek. You seem to be doing something constructive with your life and I feel as though I'm just stuck. I can't move forward.'

He turned and hugged her tightly. 'You haven't mentioned him for a long time. I thought you were getting to grips with it.'

'I don't know if you ever do. It feels as though there's a huge black hole and no amount of filling it will help. I wake up at night and hear his voice in my head telling me to be strong, as he was, and to move on, but I can't.'

'You don't have to forget him, Jana, but things change, you have to move on.'

'I need to be able to move on and make my own decisions, without this cloud over me.'

Her grief was a part of her that he could not reach.

'He's left a gap that nothing, no person, can fill. I don't

know how to get to the other side, wherever that is. The ache is always there. It tinges everything I see and do with a greyness. You're the first person I've said all of this to. I'm sorry.'

'Don't apologise. It's not too much.' He shook his head, feeling helpless. They walked through the old streets that she must have been familiar with, and he hoped that having him with her would help.

It was a balmy early autumn day and the clouds rolled across the sky above them in wisps of silver and white, like puffs of smoke. The greatness of the universe felt tangible – each person was as small as a grain of sand in the grand scheme.

'I often wonder if Tatínek is watching us,' she said. 'What would he think of my life now? Somewhere along the way I've lost anchor and I'm drifting, waiting for something. I don't even know what it is that I'm waiting for.' She threw her hands up and looked at him.

'Answers, maybe?' said Miloš.

'Life isn't what I expected it to be but, according to Matka, it rarely is.'

'Jana, I don't know what to do to help.'

She looked up at him as they walked. 'I don't know either.'

'The phone calls,' he said.

'What about them?'

'Well, is that why you didn't call much?'

'I just needed time to think.'

There was something appealing about her vulnerability. It made him want to be there. She looked beautiful, strands of her hair caught the sun. Despite her feelings, she still had a bounce as she walked. The city had given her an edge, a way of moving and speaking that was unfamiliar to him. In Letovice she had been softer. She moved in a way that made him want to follow her. He would follow her anywhere if he could just be with her and know that she felt the same way. She felt just out of reach.

Chapter 13

'Benes, great to see you.' Lukas shook his hand and they sat down at the bar. 'It's been a while. How are you?'

'Good, thanks. Tell me about you, I haven't seen you since before the wedding.'

'That long?'

They picked up their beers and surveyed the bar, the way they always did, as if they were looking for something interesting to happen.

'How was the honeymoon?'

'Ah, wonderful. The mountain air was good. It seems so long ago now.'

'And married life?' Lukas smirked, expecting them to start making jokes. 'Still allowed out?' he quipped. They laughed.

'It's actually great. We're enjoying life.'

'Glad to hear.' Lukas missed his weekly drinks with Benes,

and the banter they used to enjoy.

'So, stranger, enough about me, what's been taking up your time lately?'

'Work, mainly. We're busy with various restoration projects but I can't complain. I like it that way'

'Any lady on the scene?'

'No, not really.'

Lukas felt uncomfortable about the interrogation, and he didn't want to bring up the subject of Jana. He had no idea what was going on and it didn't seem helpful to talk about her, least of all because Benes had just married her sister. It was all too close.

'Ah, come on Lukas, you're never short of a story.'

'I don't know what you mean. I'm shocked at the insinuation.' He dropped his jaw in jest.

'There must be someone.'

'Well there isn't. Change the subject.'

Benes knew that he wasn't going to get anywhere with Lukas and he started to reminisce about the big day.

'It was a great day and she looked beautiful.

'You're a lucky man.'

Wasn't that what everyone said? You're meant to encourage your friends and tell them they've made the right choice. Lukas didn't dislike Irena, but he found her too quiet for comfortable conversation. How could she be related to the girl who had grabbed him at the fountain? He found himself asking the same question throughout their conversation. The two girls appeared to be so different, so opposite.

'Her family are great,' said Benes, 'Irena's mother and friends were so helpful with all the wedding planning. I wouldn't have known where to start.'

'Find me a man who would,' said Lukas.

'She really missed her father. She doesn't talk about him much.'

'No, neither does Jana.'

'What do you mean? You hardly know her.'

'I mean I've heard people say they both struggle with their loss.'

'I see.' Benes looked puzzled.

There was an awkward silence and Lukas knew he had replied too hastily. He should have kept his mouth shut and just listened to his friend. Instead, he had responded on impulse. Benes eventually broke the silence.

'Of course those who knew him don't want to forget him. His legacy lives on in his speeches, in his writings.'

'What do you mean?'

'He wasn't known for being a wallflower, Lukas.'

'I've never met him. I'm afraid I don't know much about him. I suppose I only really know Irena because of you.'

'He was a lecturer at the School of Economics. He was a great believer in freedom and was seen as a threat to the authorities at the time. He got to know Havel during his time in prison. He was a dissident, Lukas.'

'Prison?'

'Yes. He was arrested several times. He was there for long enough to meet others fighting for the same cause. You know

– change, revolution.'

For a moment it was as if time stood still, and for Lukas the penny had dropped.

'What was his name?'

'Radek. His name was Radek. Why do you ask?'

'No reason really, just curious.'

'He was an interesting guy, I liked him, but he was often on the wrong side of the law – a very persuasive man. He could make you believe anything.'

'That's a real gift,' said Lukas. The memories began to return, filling his thoughts like poison, thoughts of days that he believed he'd long forgotten. He could feel his body breaking into a cold sweat, but tried to contain his reactions. Benes had missed the look of surprise on his friend's face.

'A blessing and a curse, I think. His wife always worried about him. He loved his daughters. I think he was especially close to Jana. She's a bright girl. I don't think she agreed with him all the time but she certainly listened, and she could give most politicians a run for their money given the chance.'

'Really?' Lukas hoped to be able to tease more information out of his friend.

'She's certainly more talkative than her sister and she knows what she wants. Not sure I could handle someone so spirited.'

There were so many questions that he promised himself he would not ask. He was concerned about Benes discovering his link with her father. He was only just beginning to understand the full implications of this new revelation. Lukas took a deep breath, another swig of beer, and sat back in the chair.

'Why do you think she didn't go into the same line of work as her father?' He couldn't help himself. There was a thread of his nature which needed answers. It ran through every fibre of his inquisitive mind.

'I don't know. I don't think she shared his belief that changes could be made – not with a communist government.'

Lukas found it strange to hear Benes talking about Jana. It was as though someone had crashed into his private world and opened up his thoughts. The implications of Radek's relationship to Jana, the girl whose trust Lukas had gained, forced beads of sweat to the surface of his skin. His forehead felt damp with fear.

As a rule, he didn't ever reveal much information to any one person, but it was impossible to know where he would end up with this grizzly predicament. Although it was so long ago now, the new revelations were unnerving. How would he behave around Jana? What would happen if his past was to catch up with him?

'Well, I'd better head back.' Benes put his beer down on the table. 'I told Irena I'd be back about now. I haven't seen her much this week. She's been busy sorting things out for her mother, finances and things, and I've had a long week at work.'

He got up, dropped a note on the table, patted Lukas on the back and walked out into the night air.

Lukas sat in the bar and ordered a lone beer. He didn't feel ready to leave just yet, and wanted to avoid walking back with

Benes in case he said more than he should. The news of Radek had jolted him and he didn't know how to proceed.

His days of trying to avoid people – and their questions – had been firmly locked away in the back of his mind. He hadn't anticipated a resurrection of all the memories, the guilt.

Chapter 14

Miloš would be in Manila by now, possibly even on his way south to Mindanao. Their time together had been short but healing, and she felt a temporary sense of calm wash over her. Looking out of the window of the apartment, she watched the swing swaying in the wind outside and wondered if life was going to be as complicated as she feared it would.

The phone rang. The place was empty but she managed to grasp the receiver from its cradle before the ringing tone stopped.

'Jana, is that you?'

'Yes, who is it?'

'It's me, Lukas. The idiot who didn't kiss you back

'What are you talking about?'

She winced at his apology, if that's what it was. His call was too close to Miloš's departure. The fact that neither of them really knew about the other helped her to regain some sense of control over her life. It was little consolation, but it was enough.

'I'm sorry,' he continued, 'I was just taken aback, that's all. I've missed your voice.'

'It's good to hear you,' she said, hoping it would release her from the moment at the fountain.

'I wondered if you wanted to meet up.' His voice sounded shaky.

'I suppose so.'

'Only if you have the time. I know you must be busy.'

'No, it's fine. How about this Saturday? I'll meet you at Café Slavia on Narodni. Is ten OK for you?'

'Yes, good choice. I'll see you there.'

The days dragged until Saturday. Jana sensed the confusion beginning to creep in. She knew that seeing Lukas was unfair but, despite his response to her kiss, he was a mystery – a beautiful, earthy concoction of things she couldn't quite get to grips with.

She jumped off the tram one stop early and, with plenty of time, she wanted to walk. There was a sense of peace in the city she called home which had changed the atmosphere and the expressions on people's faces. There was no longer any need to live in fear or to watch your every move and guard your words. Despite the changes going on in the Czech Republic – changes she couldn't yet embrace – Jana had a sense that things were not quite over yet but she wasn't sure why.

As she reached the corner by the café, opposite the National Theatre, she was reminded of marching in the crowds with Tatínek on that cold November afternoon along Narodni. She could almost hear the footsteps and feel the vibrations of the crowds marching together. She could see the flags waving furiously – red, white, blue. She remembered her fear.

Turning the corner onto the riverside of the café, the view of the castle across the water lifted her spirits. There would never be another view like this. She drew a deep breath and pushed through the heavy wooden doors and through another set. Entering the café transported you back in time, a time where the green leather seats were graced by poets and authors fuelling their writing with coffee and scenes of the river and the castle. Scanning the tables she located Lukas sitting under the painting of the Absinthe Drinker with an espresso and a paper. He looked as though he belonged there. He smiled.

'Hi, you look good,' he said.

He got up to give her a kiss on the cheek, a greeting he thought appropriate for the time being. He wanted to hug her but he wasn't sure, so he leaned on the side of caution.

'Thank you. You've shaved.' She took her coat off and carefully looped it over the peg on the wall.

'Yes, thought it was time it went.'

He had decided to get rid of the stubble. Quite why, he wasn't sure, maybe in an attempt to expose his face. Subconsciously he wanted to expose his feelings for her and his links with her father but he couldn't, not now. He would risk losing her. Jana ordered a coffee and sat down on the chair opposite.

'I like it.'

'Really?' he wondered if she would still like him if she knew the truth.

'So how have you been? Have you seen your sister much since she's been back?'

'She's good, thanks. They had a great honeymoon.'

'I'm sorry I missed the wedding.' He folded the paper roughly and leaned in towards her.

'It seems so long ago now,' she said.

She ran her fingers around the polished metal table rims and gazed out of the window. The trams rolled over the cobbles – flashes of red and white as they picked up speed. He wondered what she was thinking, she didn't give much away. He had messed up the last time they were together. How could he get closer to her, when he had betrayed someone that she loved? He had managed to live with himself up to this point, but what kind of twist of fate had led him to her?

The stress must have started to show because he could feel a bead of sweat on his forehead. Hoping she hadn't noticed, he wiped it with his scarf and leaned back into the chair.

'Beautiful, isn't it?' he said, 'Hradčany, the rooftops, the reflections.'

'Everything,' she said, continuing his sentence. 'The light catches the water, and the reflections of the castle at this time of day are amazing.' She turned back to face him. 'How's work?'

'Busy, the mosaic is time-consuming.'

At least a mosaic, or something which was unearthed, had some sort of general pattern to it, but this situation had no code or expected outcome and he had no team to work with, no back-up. Suddenly Lukas felt small and worthless in the light of his betrayal. The worst part was that she knew nothing.

Jana continued, oblivious to his thoughts.

'I love the sound of your work. It sounds so romantic and it must be intriguing to put pieces of the past together.'

How was he supposed to piece together his days in prison with Radek and the situation he was now in with this girl – this headstrong, intelligent girl?

He wished he could scrub out the past, the way he had earlier washed the dirt off the intricate Roman tiles. The past had begun to rear its ugly head in ways he had never imagined.

'It is,' said Lukas, 'but it becomes less exciting when you're working on it every day.'

'Like any relationship.' She smiled. 'I can see why you make a good archaeologist.'

'Conservator,' he corrected her.

'Well, you've got the right look.'

'What's that got to do with it?'

He never knew how to take her directness. He found it uncomfortable. Trying to play down his job felt like a poor attempt at minimising the impact of his misconduct. If he could make his work less exciting in her eyes, he might also be able to take the edge off what he had done when the time came.

He had tried to forget but memories of the prison cell

would wake him at night. He had thought about the letter repeatedly. At the time it was his only way out and trading information had been the only method of escape. It didn't matter who you harmed. It seemed so harsh, now that it was all over but, at the time, it was a form of survival. At least that's what he had told himself.

'I think it's a noble job.'

Her innocent comment jolted him back into the present. Now she was actually making him sound virtuous. Memories of the dark days surfaced like bullets travelling towards him. He remembered begging the guard to release him. He had only been in prison for a few weeks after there had been a knock at his door in the night. They always came at night.

'Lukas?' he remembered them asking him sternly. He knew then that his days of campaigning were over. His 'activities against the state', as they called it, had brought him to this point, and his Jewish roots hadn't helped. They used any excuse they could find to haul you in.

That particular night was a blur but he remembered each day in prison vividly. He wondered if he would ever forget the lack of hope that he felt. The letter was just meant to get him out, it was his ticket to freedom. He didn't feel free now, ensnared by his own foolish actions. The consequences he had to live with obstructed the path to forming any kind of relationship with Jana. If she ever knew, or found out, he didn't think he could live with himself. It was hard enough, even with her not knowing. He looked at her soulful eyes and clean, crisp skin and shuddered at the thought of tainting her with what he had experienced through the days of the regime.

'I wouldn't say noble. People who save lives rather than destroy them, those are the people who do noble work, Jana.'

'I suppose so. You just seem to do such interesting work.'

It didn't so much matter to him what kind of work he was doing. He would have swapped interesting for noble – or plain honest, for that matter – just to feel clean, to remove the shame he lived with every moment of the day. Why had she been brought into his life and inadvertently cast into the daylight all of his shame? Was he being punished?

'People are much more interesting,' he quipped, trying to deflect the undeserved admiration.

'I just think it sounds so unique. What have you got planned for the weekend?'

'Quiet, really. Nothing special.' He couldn't see her again until he had found a solution.

'We could see a film tomorrow night?' she said.

He hesitated and agreed, wondering if he had really heard himself saying yes. Lukas was stuck somewhere between the reality of her angelic face and his dark, concealed past. How could just a letter, a small piece of paper, ruin his life and all chances of a relationship with her? Why hadn't he just waited, like the rest of the prisoners, waited for it all to end? Because it did, eventually.

Chapter 15

Lukas reached across the mosaic for a soft brush to clean the tiles. He could see a range of colours through the dirt. It was hard to imagine the beauty of a thing before it had become marred by dust and dirt and, even with restoration, nothing was quite the same as the original. As a conservator, he was under no illusion that restoration could truly bring something back to its original form.

Even with the dust brushed off an artefact, be it a clay pot or a set of mosaic tiles or a building, there would still be cracks and dents which increased over a period of time. It made life so temporary, that nothing stayed the same, that objects weathered, and that people could destroy objects and buildings or other people – even, at times, unwittingly.

He put the tiles down and made a coffee. Looking out of the small workshop window towards the river, he reflected on the situation with Jana. He knew there was no hope of a future with her, yet the idea wouldn't leave his mind. At least, not if he wanted to live a life free from any further guilt or lies.

He hadn't foreseen the ways in which the past could come back to haunt him with such crushing weight. It felt isolating, confusing and even shameful.

His mind spiraled through every consequence he could imagine. Living a lie and hiding the truth from her, which he knew would be torment, walking away, the consequences of which he would still have to live with, and facing the truth to see how she would react in the vain hope of some form of forgiveness, or at least an acceptance of what he had done. The last of the three looked so nasty in his mind's eye. He couldn't forgive himself for the loss he had caused her. It was easy to blame someone, to blame the brutality of the regime. He had always been impulsive, it was a trait he had inherited from his father. This situation had no answers. Jana was, teasingly, just out of reach.

It was a curious thing in the minds of men to want something unattainable, something forbidden. Some women had a geisha-like quality. It made them all the more interesting and presented a challenge, which had to be mastered. The thrill of the chase was often more appealing than the catch itself, as with a lion in the wild.

With no hint as to how Jana was feeling about him now, and without her knowledge of his wrongs, he lived in the hope that it might work. Maybe there was another life, or at least another chance. If he could wipe away his history, as though it had never happened, Lukas would have given anything.

Living through dark days when your every word could have been a betrayal and anyone could turn you in for something invisible, people were pushed to limits they never knew existed. You learned not to trust your neighbour, the person you met at work, or even your own family.

A friend from the same district in Prague had been taken away at night because a neighbour had tipped off the police about his support for 'Western philosophies', as they called it then. He apparently had too many Western contacts and was a possible 'threat'. Lukas's father had friends in Western Europe who sent letters and small gifts for birthdays. Each envelope or packet arrived mysteriously opened and resealed. Sometimes they didn't even bother to reseal the letters.

Prague Prison, Bartolomejska Street, 1980

'Lukas, my name's Lukas Dobransky.'

The new inmate had just arrived. He was yet to experience the beatings, the starvation, solitary confinement.

'I'm Radek Maček, I think it's just you and me in this cell.'

'It seems so.' Lukas couldn't bring himself to say much more. He felt weak and his lungs were tight.

'Why are you here?' asked the new inmate.

'I'm still trying to figure it out. I think it was something to do with family connections outside. You know, western connections.

Radek shuddered, 'Cold, isn't it? They took me in for

copying and distributing papers. I'd keep doing it if they let me out. We can't give up.'

Lukas turned to face the newcomer.

'They'll wear you down. I've been here for a few months.'

'I've left a wife and family behind. You?'

'No.' Lukas shook his head. 'Just me.'

'Well, you seem like a fine young man, Lukas.' His eyes smiled as he spoke. He had a calm manner and an enthusiasm that would only be broken down. They lay back on their thin mattresses on the lower levels of each of the two metal framed bunk beds, and looked up at the empty beds above. Radek pulled a worn blanket over his legs.

'Who else is in here?' he asked.

'Not sure. There's a playwright, Havel. He's in P-6. He's been sentenced several times. They say he's a political dissident.'

The barred window let in little light. The walls were grey, possibly meant to be white. Sometimes, in the night, Lukas would imagine that they closed in on him, crushing the life out of him.

'They shot some men yesterday,' said Lukas. 'Post arrived, they scattered it into the snow and told the men to run to get it. Those that did … they didn't return.'

The men lay in silence. Lukas could feel his heartbeat slowing.

'You see, Radek, I'm afraid. We're meant to stay strong, but I can't, not in these conditions. They break you down … mentally, physically. I can't … '

'It will be over soon. I know it will. We're not far from freedom and democracy.'

'I wish I had your certainty, your hope.'

'Nothing like this can last, not forever,' said Radek. His voice was strong and comforting.

The door flew open with a bang. They sat up abruptly. A guard placed two pieces of bread down on the stone floor and slammed the door shut. They could hear the handles turn and the bolts shoot across into the latches – the footsteps moving away, fading into the corridor. The light in the corridors were dim, haunting. The door was thick plate-metal, made to keep animals contained. Vast water pipes in the corridors kept him awake at night. Sometimes he heard screams in the distance.

***

He replayed events, again and again in his mind, in the hope of finding an alternative course that he could have taken. It wouldn't change anything – the current situation was irreversible – but it felt cathartic to at least try and find a possible way around it, had he been given the chance.

Lukas put the mug down on the window sill, leaned forward and lowered his head into his hands as if to hold the weight of his body. His temples sank down into his fingertips and he could feel his breath on his hands. He felt disconnected from the distant sounds outside, and imprisoned by his own destruction.

When the country was released from its oppressors, only

recently, they had all celebrated. No one, he thought, had imagined paying for any previous misdeeds. It was the authorities who were wrong, and the people were captives in a society where news was filtered and lives were ordered, school curriculums dictated by the state, and access to the outside world carefully monitored and restricted. How could a citizen be wrong? Surely he or she was just a pawn in a large, tightly guided game? He tried to justify, nullify, his actions by blaming the powers that once were for his decisions and his former life. It was something that the next generation would possibly never understand. Memories of the past few decades were already fading in people's minds and he wondered whether, in time, some would try to even deny that communist rule had ever existed in their homeland.

Lukas could understand Jana's dislike of change. She had lost her father to a system that stole him from her childhood and her future. Maybe she could see the disadvantages of their freedom in a way that others couldn't. Maybe it would change the culture entirely, or even the people themselves. Maybe they would lose something unique to them as a nation. When you let sunlight into a garden, she had said, plants start to grow and they seem to flourish and prosper but so, too, do the weeds and the pests. He disagreed – the future had to be better than the past.

He knew it was useless to try and appease his guilt by thinking that she wouldn't understand his actions, but he knew that he underestimated her. She was sharp, what she lacked in experience, she made up for in intuition and understanding.

She read widely and asked questions. Jana hadn't become biased by her father's views, and Lukas respected her for that. He respected her for many reasons. She knew her own mind, and it was one of her appealing qualities that he found captivating. Lukas had never respected anyone who hung on to his every word, without their own opinion.

He could see nothing but good in the kind of freedom they were now experiencing, although his knowledge and understanding of life outside the Eastern bloc was limited until the recent revolution, a day which Jana's father had talked about, almost prophetically, from within the cell walls. A prison cell forced you to consider life, failed opportunities, time wasted. He shuddered at the thought of ever being in the same position again. The sense of worthlessness and loss that he experienced had torn him apart until the day when he accepted his fate and started to lose hope. It wasn't until the idea came to him to write to the authorities that he could see a window of opportunity.

The rain came down on the river in the distant view, first of all in a patter, then in a raging torrent. It had been a while since the rain had fallen. The air always smelled different when the ground was damp. Opening the window slightly, he breathed in the city air and watched the leaves dance as they were struck by the droplets. They turned and bounced back as if shying away from him.

People in the street in front struggled to open umbrellas but the force of the gale was too strong and they ran for cover.

Mothers sheltered their children and the odd stray cat had long escaped the downpour. Lightning flashed and he waited for the thunder.

His father taught him that the gap between the lightning and the thunder told you the distance between you and the storm, but he couldn't remember the exact calculations. The thunder clapped almost simultaneously and he knew it was close. The intensity of the rain heightened and he watched the chaos outside, enjoying the safety of his workroom. The storm had arrived quickly, triggering a memory of a conversation in a café. Jana had tried to warn him of the impending spiral of changes that were to come if they welcomed this 'freedom' as a country just emerging from its chrysalis. She had spoken of the need for protection from greed and power. The only way that it could be described, she said, was as a storm hitting a field which had become dry in the heat of the sun and something about a thirst for rain. Lukas watched the river flowing in the distance and tried to remember the details. Perhaps, somewhere along the line, he had learned to block them out. His work involved precision but it was easier to restore an inanimate object than to reveal your soul.

He remembered. She said that when the ground had become dry, and was in desperate need of water, when the rains came it wasn't able to absorb the water. The majority would run off into rivers and leave the ground thirsty. It was as if the very need itself, the release from dryness, was creating an inability to receive.

Chapter 16

Jana arrived at the government building for her interview, having decided on a career change. She had told the school in Letovice that she would not be going back. An advertisement in the paper had caught her eye. She felt inspired by this new opportunity and wanted to involve herself in something that would help to understand what the revolution had sought to change.

'Must have an enquiring mind and be able to efficiently research and collate information,' read the job description. Her limited office experience would lower her chances, but Jana wanted to take the risk.

Knocking on the door of the director's office reminded her of visits to the school principal as a child. With trepidation, you would knock and wait until the person was ready to receive you.

It was a simple wooden door with the director's name on a plaque. As she entered the room Jana saw Havel's portrait on the wall behind his head. It was difficult to imagine that this man had met her father in prison all those years ago. At one time they must have wondered whether they would ever be freed.

If life could have told her what was to come – the fate of her father in the years beyond – she wouldn't have wanted to know. It was hard to imagine why anyone would want to see into their future when, at times, it was bleak. Why would you want to know if you would succeed or fail, or whether you would live or die? It was a bizarre idea and one which would occupy her thoughts for the next few seconds.

'Jana?' Mr Soucek stood up and greeted her with a brisk handshake. He reminded her of one of her old schoolteachers, the mathematics teacher – well dressed and neatly turned out. He was just the sort of person to be interviewing her. His manner was curt and decisive. He had a brusque way of moving the conversation forward and hurrying her through the procedures. There were procedures for almost every event when it came to government operations. He gestured for her to take a seat opposite. As she looked around the room, he tidied some papers and removed a coffee mug, leaving a grey smudged ring stain on the colourless desk. There was very little furniture apart from the obvious. His computer was positioned on the edge of the desk to the left and the chair was plain and upright. *He* was plain and upright.

A framed picture rested against the shelves behind his

chair. From what she could see it was possibly a holiday snap of his two children. The rows and rows of government policy booklets lined the shelves below, along with a variety of books on political history and some information on statistics.

The sun shone through a dusty window and the blinds looked as though they had never left the ceiling. It was difficult to see how they could be rolled down, the thread looked too short to reach.

'Now,' he said, 'what can you tell me about yourself?'

Jana braced her mind for the barrage of questions that she had expected. She prepared a few answers the night before but felt certain that it wasn't going to adequately cover the areas required.

'I'm a Czech citizen residing in Prague. I'm interested in helping to research for your cases.'

'Yes, I think you wrote about your reasons for applying for this job in your letter. Tell me, why is it that having trained in physiotherapy you are now seeking to work with us?'

The tone of his voice gave away a hint of suspicion and, for a moment, she felt as though she was about to be interrogated for entering the room. It felt more to her like a general question about life than a specific investigation of her curriculum vitae. Jana wondered where this was leading and drew a breath quietly before responding.

'Mr Soucek, as much as I have enjoyed my career so far, I really do want to help with the research in this exciting post-revolutionary period. I can touch-type and I have a lot of experience with computer programs.'

'I see,' he responded, sounding unconvinced by her answer.

She had started at a young age, sitting next to Tatínek as he wrote coding and formatting for various projects. Mr Soucek was unlikely, though, to be impressed by this early learning. It was irrelevant to him. It's relevance to her lay in the time that she and her father had spent together. She absorbed much of what she knew from his brilliance.

'I have been keeping up to date with all the events for as long as I can remember, and I know how much work still needs to be done.'

'And your parents? What is it that they do?'

'My mother was a librarian until she had a family and my father used to be a lecturer at the university.'

'Hmm, and what does he do now?'

'I'm afraid he passed away.'

There was a moment of silence, then Mr Soucek responded with the kind of emotion that she hadn't expected from a man with such deadpan expressions. He lifted his chin up from looking at the notes on his desk and spoke purposefully.

'I'm sorry to hear that. We just need to know what your...persuasions are, you see.'

'Yes, yes, I understand.'

'May I ask what his subject was?'

'Yes, he worked in the Faculty of Economics. He was an advocate for change and for democracy. It got him into trouble many times.'

'Thank you, we found from our records that he had been imprisoned, but it is sometimes difficult to tell who has been incriminated and why.'

'I know and it's a record which doesn't get wiped clean. I am just grateful that he lived with the conviction, which drove him to inspire change in people's minds. Even more so, that he lived to see an end to it.'

'For a lady of your age I'm surprised you are so interested in all of this.'

'I grew up with it so it's difficult not to take notice.'

They surveyed each other carefully. Jana drew in another deep breath as if to prepare herself for the next set of questions. With the feeling that her father's work may have paved the way for her, she was quietly hopeful that they would hire her.

'Well, I can see that you are determined and your references are certainly encouraging.' She remembered asking a previous employer, at the clinic in Prague where she had worked, for references, but was amazed that they had been contacted so quickly. He stood up, leaned across the desk, and reached out to shake her hand firmly.

'Thank you, Mr Soucek. Thank you for your time.'

The clock hands had moved without her noticing. Leaving the building was like leaving a huge vault. There were endless corridors, with doors around every corner. It was difficult to know if you were heading towards the exit or just walking in circles. The interior was stark and clinical. It had all the qualities of a hospital ward and all the character of a morgue.

Jana imagined the vast rooms full of files containing sensitive material that had been concealed from the public eye.

Although the government had changed hands, she wondered how many sympathisers still currently worked amongst them.

She had read that between December 1989 and March 1990, over fifty per cent of all members of parliament had been replaced with the current majority of non-communists. The first article, which had been removed from the constitution, prescribed the leading role of the Communist Party

The changes were gradual but over time a democracy was to be built, and constitutional changes led to the birth of the newly formed Czech and Slovak Republics within the former Czechoslovakia. She had done her homework and was well informed.

Jana reached the exit and received a nod from the security guard whom she had seen on the way in. It was good to finally be out in the fresh air. Looking into the river she could see the reflection of the castle, and Jana imagined scenes which had been reflected in these waters through the long course of their country's history. Had the people walking to the marches in the Velvet Revolution been seen in the river's reflections? Those who were involved in the Prague Spring? Had it seen those who were escorted out of their homes late at night? Had these streets seen the secret police following 'dissidents'?

Now part of a republic, the city had witnessed so much oppression prior to reaching the freedom, which many were now so vehemently defending. Jana had only her childhood memories and Tatínek's stories, but she was more afraid of the future than the past. She could not wholeheartedly embrace the present, something prevented her from doing so. It was like being attached to a long piece of elastic, which drew her back to where she started each time. The words her father had often spoken echoed in her mind throughout the interview.

'Find your passion, keep hope steadfast in your mind, then sacrifice everything.'

There had been something about the advertisement that had given her the impetus to apply. She had a curiosity about the past and the records, which made this particular vacancy stand out from the others.

'You can spend your life fighting for a cause without seeing what's right in front of you.' This was his other saying. Jana had a rough idea of what he meant. He used to speak in riddles and he would say everything with such conviction that she found it, at times, unnerving.

His words haunted her in the months following his death – as though there was something of his spirit left behind, propelling her forwards. Jana hadn't voiced these thoughts to anyone, but she sensed a need for her to carry on the work that he had sweated over tirelessly.

The hours when they had stayed up talking were now crystalising the many ideas in her mind, and overcoming her doubts. She was trapped between her resistance to this new freedom and the nagging words of her father to never give up.

Chapter 17

Lukas settled on the sofa with a cool beer and breathed in the scent of the air, infused with the blossom from the trees outside the building. This was possibly his favourite time of year, reminding him of school days when they looked forward to spending time outside.

Lukas had been keen to work on the cathedral mosaic from the outset, and was glad to assist in setting up the monitoring station at the castle. He had become part of the working group for the masterpiece because* of his experience with mosaic preservation. In preparation for the interview the following morning, he had to make sure that there were no gaps in his knowledge. He would be asked difficult questions about the history of the mosaic and previous restorative techniques.

Articles and books were scattered across the coffee table in a way that made them look as though he had been reading for hours, days even. He was just about to begin when the phone rang.

'Hi Lukas.' Jana's voice sounded breezy. 'How are you?'

He hadn't expected a call from her but he needed to hear her voice again.

'Good, thanks.'

'What are you up to?'

'I'm just preparing for a press interview.'

Their conversations were often picked up after a gap of a few weeks. Lukas longed for a time when she could be sitting with him in the evenings and they'd sit in silence and read. He hadn't been in a comfortable relationship, or any relationship at all, for some time.

'Yes, Benes mentioned that when I last saw him.'

He suspected that much of his news was being relayed to her and wished that he knew of her movements while they were apart. He missed hearing her thoughts.

'I probably don't need to tell you much more,' he said.

'No, he didn't say much, just that you were busy.'

Lukas felt as apprehensive about the interview tomorrow as he did every time he spoke to her. It was as if he was about to be caught out.

'I just have a lot of reading to do. I have an interview with a radio station tomorrow morning.'

'I'll be quick. I just wondered if you were free this week.'

He'd missed her so much it was hard to say no, despite the workload and his apprehension. His head told him to walk away, but he couldn't. He felt compelled to see her. He couldn't let her go, not yet.

'How about Thursday?' he said.

'Great, I'll see you at the bar on the corner of Wenceslas Square.'

'Sure, let's say eight.'

'Good, see you then.'

She hung up. He sat back with the papers and started to read. His train of thought was frequently interrupted with thoughts of Jana. He had missed the sound of her voice. There was something that made him feel he needed her.

He pushed the quandary of their relationship, or lack of it, to the back of his mind and decided to concentrate on the task in hand. The thick white head of beer rested on the resin-coloured liquid that was to quench his thirst and calm his nerves for the remaining few hours of the evening. He swallowed the first mouthful and put his feet up with the reams of papers that demanded his attention. He ran his fingers through his hair and tapped his foot on the wood floor. It made a satisfying sound. He thought of her.

He looked at the main points – the Golden Gate, the south-facing entrance to St. Vitus's Cathedral. It had displayed the gilded mosaic of the Last Judgement since the reign of Charles IV, the Bohemian king and Roman emperor. Work had begun in 1370 and was inspired by his trips to Italy. This part of the history he knew but it was the fine detail, which needed to be memorised. The mosaic had only taken a year to complete and, given the complexity of the design, this was an astounding feat. The individual pieces of stone incorporated in the mosaic were made in over thirty different colours. Despite fifteenth-century restoration – which, in his view, had been quite soon after completion – the work had become almost invisible.

As the hours rolled by he read paper after paper and tried to imagine the workers constructing this mammoth task with limited resources, compared to the tools that were used today.

His eyes felt heavy, and the beer had helped him to unwind. Lukas headed towards his bedroom. There was never a moment that he could remember, between his head reaching the pillow and waking again each night, hours later. Those were the moments that he dreaded, when the light was barely there – moments filled with fear and anxiety, and with memories.

The following morning was filled with briefings before the press interview. It was to be broadcast by several local and national radio stations and kept in the castle archives with the rest of the material on the project. It was important to record as much information as possible.

As he walked in through the castle gates and past the guards, Lukas thought about the task ahead of them. It was a project for experts. He was an expert, not in people, but in conservation and preservation. He wished he had learned how to preserve trust and loyalty. These were the details that really mattered.

He was flattered that they had asked him to take part in the project, and was keen to research the history. There had been many meetings where he had noted the important points that he would require this morning. The mosaic was so valuable and fragile. It was in such a state of disrepair that he couldn't envisage its restored state. It was a task which was both necessary and insurmountable. On arriving in the pressroom, microphones were thrust at him from every direction.

'Mr Dobransky, this is one of the finest examples of monumental medieval mosaic art in Europe. What can you tell us about the methods of restoration that will be used to preserve the tiles?'

He nodded, looking across the room at the sea of photographers and journalists. The microphones spread around him like birds waiting to be fed. He predicted that just a tiny morsel would leave them hankering after more.

'I am proud to be able to contribute to this. It is an important project and will require years of work. This is just the beginning. We are in the embryonic stages and need to develop a strategy for restoring the glass tiles. We have the best team from all of the key specialist areas.'

'What is the scale of the work?'

'There are almost a million cubes of glass. It is eighty-four square metres in area, so you can imagine the amount of work involved.'

'Thank you. What's caused the large-scale damage?'

The reporters shuffled around, trying to get a good view of him and scribbling notes. Photographers angled themselves to get the best shots and flashes darted across the room from different directions. Lukas fiddled with the bottom of his shirt, which was hanging out loosely over his trousers.

'The problem is that the glass is made from potash, which is potassium-based and is not as strong as sodium-based glass. It was difficult to access soda when the mosaic was originally made so the potassium carbonate was extracted from burned wood ash.'

'Can you tell us more about the corrosive damage?'

'Yes, when the potash glass tiles get wet the sodium leaks and reacts with pollutants in the air. This has caused widespread damage and we need to find a way of coating it to protect the work from further corrosion once it has been cleaned.'

'Mr Dobransky, that's quite a job. What range of expertise do you have on the team?'

'Well, I feel honoured to be asked to join the group. We are working with leading Czech art historians, scientists and conservators.' Some of the men were jostling to reach the front of the scrum.

'Are there any pieces missing?'

'Yes, we need to find a way of replacing them as part of the restoration work.'

Lukas glanced at his watch, wondering how long the questions would continue, but was relieved to discover that the questions were relatively straightforward. They just wanted the background, a canvas upon which to hang the information they chose to air or print.

There were press reporters taking notes but the radio broadcasters were the most aggressive in their questioning. The microphones hovered close to his mouth, as if he was about to give them the all-important nugget.

It was a nerve-racking experience and he wondered, for a moment, why he had been chosen, given that many of the others were just as knowledgeable and experienced. He wasn't entirely confident in this situation. A journalist burst through his thoughts with another question.

'Why is this particular mosaic so important to the cathedral and, indeed, to the country?'

He looked up at the ceiling, trying to construct a coherent response.

'It is, without question, one of the most important medieval examples of a very particular technique in this region. Unfortunately, though, the corrosion occurred at such a rate that by the late nineteenth century it was in a bad state. It had been restored very early on and repeatedly, but the damage has been aggressive.'

'Wasn't there a storm in 1890?'

'Yes, it damaged the mosaic so badly that it had to be removed and restored by specialists from Venice. Stonemasons worked for two months and cut it into two hundred and seventy four pieces. The panels were brought into the storeroom beneath Vladislav Hall.'

'When was it placed back over the southern entrance to the cathedral?' The questions gathered pace.

'In 1910, but by 1953 a study had been prepared to clean and regild the mosaic, then to layer it with a special coating. It would have needed regular restoration to prevent further deterioration.'

'Thank you for your time, Mr Dobransky,' the spokesperson interceded. 'We'll just take one last question from the press.'

A man at the back asked the final question.

'The Last Judgement is quite a title. Do you think it reflects the mosaic accurately?'

Not knowing how to answer the question, Lukas thought carefully for a moment before responding. 'It represents God's final judgement and is a subject which was often represented in Italian art during that period. I think all of our lives are judged, in one way or another, so there is something for people to take away with them from the scene.'

He scanned the room, which revealed a few raised eyebrows and the odd nod of a head. Making a sharp exit, he walked towards the door and out into the sunlight.

'Lukas.' The voice behind him might have been a reporter. He shuddered to think which of the many reporters could be following him, and slowly turned around. To his relief, it was Benes.

'I heard about your interview and decided to try and listen in.'

Lukas was surprised that his friend was interested in his work, and flattered that he had made the effort to come.

'How did you get in?'

'Oh, I just listened from the door. Everyone was so busy questioning you and security were OK with me being there, so I stood outside.'

'Thank you, it's good to see a familiar face after that

interrogation.'

'You handled it pretty well. I'm not sure that I would have enjoyed it.'

'It's over now and they have what they want, hopefully.' They walked side by side, and out through the main gates.

'No wonder you've been so difficult to pin down over these last few weeks. I didn't realise how much work you had on with this project. The mosaic is so beautiful. How long is it going to take to restore?'

'Years – ten, maybe twelve. We're just at the beginning.'

'Are you free for lunch? I'm walking into town,' said Benes.

'What time is it?' Lukas glanced at his watch. 'One. Yes, why not? I'll head back to work after that.'

They wandered down the steps of Zamecke Schody and along Nerudova towards the river.

Chapter 18

Charles Bridge was a familiar and inviting part of the city. It reminded Lukas of novels he had read as a boy. The sunlight caught the tops of the imposing statues along either side, and he wondered how many saints had been carved out to stand on the heights of this majestic river crossing.

Lukas viewed so much of the city's architecture as a heritage that was to be preserved and enjoyed. It came with the territory. Everything needed to be either unearthed or preserved. He was terrified of the past being uncovered and he desperately needed to preserve what little dignity he had left.

It was a situation he had never dreamed of facing, but life was a string of surprises, regrets and promise. He felt he was leading a precarious double life. All his energy was consumed by the need to suppress the thoughts that haunted him continually.

He would often wake in the night in a cold sweat thinking he was still in the small, damp cell. His palms would be clammy and, for those first few seconds, he would be convinced that he still had to find a way out, even if it involved bribery or coercion.

Lukas looked up at the statue of St Vitus and wondered why this character, dressed as a Roman legionary, hadn't fallen prey to the lions that now encased him in a freeze-framed grimace.

'What do you think of this?' said Lukas, not expecting an answer. His friend appeared to be a million miles away. 'It's different from the others I think, smaller,' said Benes.

'Do you like it?'

'Yes. They're all quite imposing. Each saint has a very different expression on his face.'

'I hadn't looked at the faces.' Lukas squinted as he looked up, the sun's rays illuminating the outlines of the saints, each one towering over the bridge like a stone army.

'I think it's strange that he was portrayed as a martyr, yet the lions never devoured him.'

'What's the story behind it?'

'He used to heal the sick and perform miracles and his reputation led him to the emperor to heal his son, but he later refused to make a sacrifice to the Roman gods.'

'How do you know all of this?' asked Lukas.

'I learned about it at school, or read a book about it ... I can't remember.'

'So is that when he was thrown to the lions?'

'Yes,' Benes continued, 'they thought he was a sorcerer, so he was put in a den of lions, but they licked him and let him ride on their backs.'

The two walked and talked as they crossed the bridge. They walked past the artists and musicians – the same tired man playing his violin, the regular glass-pipe players rubbing their fingers in a circular motion around the rims. Glass, filled with varying amounts of water, produced unusual, ethereal sounds, unlike anything Lukas had heard before. People were selling trinkets and he wondered whether in time more tourists would set foot in the city.

Lukas turned towards his friend. 'I need to talk to you, Benes,' he said.

'I thought that was exactly what we were doing.'

'I mean there's something I need to say.'

'Go on.' Benes sounded flustered.

'Years ago, before the revolution, I was imprisoned.' The last word filled his mind.

'I know, Lukas. I know you've been in some sort of trouble, but that's all in the past.'

'No, it's not.' Lukas put his hand on his friend's shoulder as if to pull him back. 'I need to tell you what happened.' Benes turned his gaze away from the river and they locked eyes for a moment which felt too long for comfort.

'I was desperate to get out of prison, and to be free again. The stench was terrible, people became ill and died, we were beaten. One night I couldn't sleep and I lay awake looking at the ceiling of the cell. There was a tiny crack in the wall and as

I stared at it, I thought about the chinks in the 'system.' There must be ways around it. I'd heard that some people had traded information for their release, but I never thought I could stoop to those depths.'

'What happened?' They stood, motionless, on the bridge.

'It's amazing what desperation does to your soul and your mind. It changes the way you make decisions. You become another person.'

Lukas wondered if those who had never experienced prison could ever understand the desperation that he was talking about. He couldn't believe he was trying to justify his actions. It was pitiful.

'I spoke to one of the guards. I mean I tried to …'

'Go on,' Benes insisted.

Lukas grasped at the words as though they were trying to run away. His heart quickened and his chest tightened. He couldn't find a way of confessing to his friend without it sending shock waves through his body. Why was he telling Benes? Maybe he needed some sort of pardon. He felt compelled to tell someone, anyone, just to be free from the secrecy. He was locked in a prison of memories and guilt, a prison that threatened to consume the present.

'I just needed to get out, but I didn't...'

'What?'

'I didn't know how bad it would get.'

'I don't understand.'

'When you told me about the girls' father, Radek, I suddenly realised who he was.'

Benes eyes were piercing and questioning.

'Irena, Jana, their father. He was a fellow prisoner, Benes.'

'We all knew people had been arrested but nobody knew why.'

'It's not the arrest that was the issue. I found a guard who was less harsh than most. I was put in one of the worst cells with the political prisoners. That's when I met him, Radek. He would lecture us on the ways of democracy when the guards weren't listening and share his views, his 'insights'. He was a wise man.'

'You met him in prison?' Benes looked incredulous.

'I did. When you spoke about him, about how the girls miss him, I could only think of what I'd done to his life, to their lives.'

'I don't understand.'

'I'd heard that the government would release you if you switched. If you gave them information, if you turned, became an informant, sold your soul. They exchanged that information for your release.'

'So what did you give them?'

'It's complicated, but I wrote a letter implicating him in a plot to overthrow the government on his release. He wasn't really involved, but I thought the government would believe that he could.'

Benes raised his eyes. 'Have you told anyone? Of course you haven't.'

'No, not until now. I managed to bury it as though it had never happened. If you pretend something doesn't exist you can convince yourself of almost anything, until it comes back to haunt you.'

'In ways you never imagine. I can't believe by some twist of fate that you've met him again in the form of his daughter. Fallen in love with her, even.'

'I wrote the letter in the laundry room and hid it until it was ready to go. Then I slipped it to one of the guards. I hoped I could trust him to pass it on to the authorities, but you never know. You don't know who you can trust or for how long.'

They stared at each other for a moment in disbelief. Benes looked shocked.

'I'd been on a hunger strike for days. Some self-harmed. You could see the new scars…if they survived. Being confined in those conditions…it's impossible to explain.'

'I had no idea.'

'No one did…no one did. It was a silent, hidden nightmare, day after day. 'You grow weak and something inside you slowly dies until you lose the will to live, to look into the future and imagine any kind of freedom.'

'But a hunger strike?'

'Benes, you can't imagine what that kind of incarceration is like.'

They slumped to the floor with their backs against the wall, one after the other. People passed by, stopping to look at the army overhead, stopping to watch street artists and listen to glass bells. Benes put his arm around his Lukas's shoulder.

'What I don't understand,' said Benes, 'is what you were doing in prison in the first place. I mean they must have had a reason, even if it was a false claim.'

'That's just it. They made vast, unproven claims about dissidents just to remove them from the streets and from society. So that they couldn't poison people's minds with the truth. People who spoke out were a threat to their regime. Fear created the control in the system. It would start with whispers, speculation, and then you would get a knock at the door or just be taken from the streets.'

'It happened to people in our street,' said Benes.

Lukas battled the scenes in his mind, as they spiralled towards him.

'I'd set up a student group to discuss ways of liberating society from totalitarianism. I was subverting the government and, under their rules, I was working against the regime. A dissident, a label which stood for all that they were against.'

'Were you involved in the silent marches during the revolution?'

'Yes. Do you remember the student who was killed by the police in the demonstration?'

'Yes,' said Benes, 'I can still remember people's reactions – horror, disbelief, shock.'

'The secret service was alleged to have used an agent called Ludvik Zifcak as the dead student Martin Smid. They faked his death. The question is, why?'

Benes rubbed his head as if to find some form of inspiration.

'You see, my friend, no one knows what part in the fall of the regime the secret service played. To be fair, no one really knew anything about the deep workings of their grip on society, like a machine.' Lukas wondered how much Benes understood.

'I've been trying to gather support for years.'

'You're a bold man. I kept my head down out of fear.'

'I'm not sure it was boldness,' said Lukas. 'Sometimes I think it was stupidity. I was tired of the dictatorship, I just couldn't sit back and wait. I couldn't wait for something to happen, or for someone else to do something. There were nights in prison where I would dream of being in another country, a country that was free. But we needed freedom in our own country.'

'You're impulsive, Lukas.'

'Looking back I still wonder if I did the right thing. I lost so much.'

'Lost?'

'My dignity when I was in prison, my freedom, and now, Jana. The guards treated us like vermin. The torrent of verbal abuse made you worthless in their eyes.'

'We never knew what was going on inside,' said Benes, 'or who was even there.'

'You wouldn't, everything was done in secret. That's what gave them so much power. I had to sign a declaration on release.'

'What sort of declaration?'

'I can still remember the wording. I think it's been imprinted on my mind ever since:

I shall remain silent regarding all the facts I have become acquainted with within the corrective-educational establishment.

The words stuck in his throat.

'So that's what they called it? Educational?'

'Apparently. The declaration finished with one sentence:

I am aware that by revealing these facts I am committing a criminal offence and I will be liable to prosecution.'

'What happened to those who refused? Did anyone refuse?'

'From what I understand they did, and were transferred to a pre-detention cell, which was worse. The rest, I don't know.'

'Liberation doesn't mean the same thing for everyone,' said Lukas, 'but to those who saw the worst of the oppression, it reminded them of their reason for fighting.'

'So, what happened once you had handed over the letter?'

'Some time later – you lost track of time inside – a guard opened my cell door. He was someone I hadn't seen before and I suspected that he didn't even work there. He nodded and told me that I was free, then I was ushered into a room and given a briefing. I'm sure he was a secret service agent masquerading as a guard. You never really knew, but it was just a hunch.'

'Briefing?' Benes asked, looking disquieted by the revelations. His mind was opening to the workings of a sinister world.

'Yes, the briefing included the signing of the declaration. They told me the sort of information to look for and how to report back. I was to receive information in a secure form on various occasions and I knew I'd be bugged.

'Phone calls?'

'Every conversation with a friend. I was meant to seek out enemies of the state specifically to trap them. The so-called freedom I was now being given came at a price. It was more of a short-term pardon. I just had to play into their hands until the country could find a way of overthrowing the system as we knew it.'

'We heard rumours, but nobody really knew.'

'That's the point, no one was meant to know that they were being watched or targeted. I still lived in fear of making mistakes, or of someone at a higher level deciding they couldn't trust me. Some of my friendships obviously had to change but no one was to suspect anything, so I had to play it carefully. It was a tightrope walk, but it was either a life lived as a puppet, controlled by strings from an invisible power, or a return to being inside.'

'How have you managed to live with the letter? How can you put all of it behind and just carry on? Will you tell Jana?'

'I don't know. I have no idea.'

'Well, you've told me, so at some point surely you'll have to tell her. You can't get into a relationship, not like this.'

Lukas ran his hands through his hair and contemplated the fact that he had already started something with her. It was too late to reverse, and he didn't want it to stop. Was this some sort of revenge from a higher power, showing him that you reap what you sow? A judgement, perhaps, or some sort of karma? He had never really believed in any kind of a God and had been taught to take control of his own destiny by his father, despite his mother's insistence on a Jewish upbringing. Was control over your own destiny even possible? It was an unusual philosophy in a world where they had had little control.

Benes played with an old piece of paper, extracted from his pocket earlier in the conversation. Lukas knew his friend was right, that he had to be honest and present her with the truth, as if he were the defendant and she the jury, but he couldn't face the pain it would cause her. The conversation risked shifting the dimensions of their friendship. Benes would soon feel like an accomplice in a crime, and Lukas as though he was stepping down from the dock to await his sentencing terms.

'So,' Benes began, 'what's the next step, my friend?'

This final question left Lukas feeling that it was all over, that he had to let go of something to be free.

'You say it as though either I need to move or you will.'

'No, the opposite. What you do with your information and your relationships is up to you. I know nothing.'

Chapter 19

Jana's new job fulfilled the needs of her inquisitive mind and she was able to use the study skills she had always relished. It felt as though something was being given back to the country at a time when so much had been snatched away.

The hours were reasonable and she was able to walk home over the bridge and along the river, frequently stopping in Wenceslas Square for a coffee and time spent with a good book. Jana felt at home in Prague. She no longer felt haunted by the death of her father and confused by the men in her life. They had drifted in and out of the scene like leaves falling in the wind.

Her work gave her a new sense of independence. Miloš's absence had provided the distance she needed and she only saw Lukas every few weeks. Mr Soucek was pleased with her work and she was religiously going through file after file looking for information. She would log what was on paper in the files and transfer it to the computer on her small corner desk. It was important to check for leading information on possible sympathisers of the regime. This information would aid government security and reveal any hidden records.

The lustration laws that had come into play in recent years had increased the government's work of sifting out former communists and secret police informants to restrict their power within the successor government and civil service positions. Their employment in positions of public office – the judiciary, the central bank, academia, army, security and procuracy – was now banned.

Jana had been warned of the risks of record-tampering and wrongful accusations from the former government. She had undergone training in this area, and her work was checked by more senior staff. It was a steep but interesting learning curve, and it challenged her skills.

She wondered what Tatínek would think about the job. She suspected he would have been less interested in government security and more concerned about the rights of those wrongly accused.

The exclusion of those most experienced in their jobs, she had been told, was problematic. Jana had been sworn to secrecy over the file content. The vault where they were kept had several security codes. There was something exciting about working with delicate information.

This purging of the country's past, as she saw it, was healing. The Czech Republic in its newest form had escaped the court trials of other former communist countries. The priority, she had been told, was to clean out the past workings of the government and not to deal with injustice at this early stage.

The evidence sat in mottled grey box files in row upon row of metal shelving, shelves on runners that were accessed by huge levers, each with three arms, bolted to the ends of the units. Inside each box there were tightly packed layers of cream folders containing papers with frayed edges. Each file was numbered with the date and signature of the agent who had taken the binding oath of collaboration.

Jana picked up the first file in the box in front of her and looked at the digits written in black pen – A5679/-048. The A stood for agent, they were known only by number – a mass of numbers in a web of information. There were records of lodgings against others, records of people's movements and contacts. Her co-worker, Pavel, told her that the blacked out names on some of the files had occurred towards the end of the communist era, possibly out of panic. Many classified files had been shredded or withdrawn. He told her that some were sent to the Soviet Union. She looked at the metal metropolis of steel disappearing into the distance – over seventeen kilometres of betrayal – and she began to see what her father had been fighting against. Much as she wanted things to stay the same, Jana couldn't ignore the raw facts – evidence of a system, which monitored, informed, controlled.

'Jana?' said Katerina. She had been working with Jana for the past month.

'I was miles away. Sorry, I didn't see you.'

'How are you getting on?' she asked. Her voice lilted as she spoke.

'Good, thanks, there's a lot of work to be done.'

'I know, people don't understand how detailed it all has to be.'

'When I arrived I was daunted by all the training, but I think I'm getting used to the job.'

Katerina and Jana had joined each other for lunch over the past two weeks. Katerina was a help when it came to learning how to process the files and understand the reams of government protocol.

Katerina was a small, neatly presented girl with sleek, dark hair and crystal-green eyes. She made Jana feel scruffy. Her brown trousers and ruffled shirts didn't have the sharp edge of Katerina's streamlined outfits. Her eye for detail and methodical mind helped her to trawl through the files with precision. They discussed some of their findings, though they were careful not to be too open about it in the cafeteria in case it was seen as unprofessional.

'You'd never hear a doctor discussing a patient in a waiting room,' Katerina had once told her. Instead, they confined talk on the sensitive issues to an empty office when no one was around.

'Is there anything you've come across this week that I can help you with?'

Jana was relieved to finally be nearing the end of the week and the weekend was in sight. She tried to think back over the current week. She would often ask Pavel, but Katerina knew there were questions that you didn't like to ask those who were more senior, for fear of looking incompetent.

'No, I think I'm OK, but thanks for asking.'

'My, we are getting to grips with it all.'

Jana wasn't sure whether or not Katerina was being patronising. She chose to believe that it was a compliment and put her mug down to add milk.

'I think it's becoming more familiar. I'm sure there will be other questions though, so I'll get back to you. I'm looking forward to getting through the next few hours before I clock off for the weekend.'

'Doing anything special?' Katerina asked.

'No, just seeing friends.'

She hadn't seen Lukas for weeks and was in need of a friendly face. Katerina was helpful and friendly enough, but they hadn't known each other for long and Lukas was a different kind of company to her work acquaintances. Jana found it a challenge meeting people in the office and having to retrain her mind and her way of working. Lukas anchored her and gave her a sense of perspective. She appreciated his carefree attitude to life, he lifted her spirits.

'Have a good weekend,' said Katerina. 'I'll catch you on Monday. Lunch?' she asked, as if Jana was difficult to pin down.

Katerina liked routine, and they usually had lunch on a Monday, although they had started to break the Monday rule, and ate together on Wednesday and Friday. As long as there was a system to it, Katerina was happy. Jana wondered how Katerina would react if she had asked to meet on a Thursday, but Matka had taught her to respect other people's wishes. Maybe that was what had made her cautious, maybe she would always have been cautious. It would have been better to be more like Tatínek, and not to have to worry about what other people thought. Each person is born with a certain set of attributes, he had said, the rest have to be learned, and worked at, to change the parts that make you less happy or comfortable. Maybe, though, they can't be changed and you are who you are, and that's it.

'Sure, see you on Monday.'

Jana jumped off the seat by the café area and sauntered down the corridor to her office. Pavel was sitting at his desk and rarely looked up when she walked into the room. The room itself was stark, much the same as all of the other small cubicles. Her desk was basic and sat neatly next to the window. The view of the city was breath-taking. On a clear day she could see for miles and, when the workload was heavy, she would gaze out across the rooftops and admire the skyline – the spires, the water, the rooftops. It was the same view that the president would see from the western side of the castle building. When the sun shone in through the window it lit up the room. The particles of dust danced across the beams of light before they settled on the furniture, or on one of the photographs or files on the shelves.

Pavel was a small, quiet and serious man. His job involved more than just the data input. He was one of the officers in charge of certain sets of files. He would weed out files that needed more careful examination and pass on to her the ones which required lower security clearance. She acquired his cast-offs. At least, that was the way she looked at it.

The end of the afternoon arrived too slowly. Once Jana had shut down the computer she raised her hand to gesture a goodbye and left the room. The labyrinth of corridors to the exit was becoming more familiar to her. The guards would nod as she left the building, and the fresh air and the crowds in the streets reminded her that civilisation outside the castle was alive.

She was getting used to the job but there was something about searching through so much history, and analysing the files of people she had never met, and would never meet, which made her crave a slice of real life at the end of the day. From nine to six she felt as though she was in a strange time warp. It was a surreal experience digging into the past when the past also involved memories of Tatínek, of his stories and of life.

Sometimes she stumbled across files of people who she thought must have had the same conviction, the same craving for a form of democracy. She began to wonder whether her fears of change were unfounded. Although only a few years had passed since the revolution, in some ways it felt as if a lifetime had been lived since that day.

Chapter 20

'Jana, you look stunning,' Lukas remarked as he walked towards her. 'I saw you walking this way, and thought I'd wait.'

'Is this the right restaurant?' she asked, looking at the small door on the corner of the street.

'I thought you'd like it. The food is good and it's atmospheric, don't you think?'

'Yes, sounds good.'

He placed his hand on the small of her back and led her into the smoky entrance.

'I've reserved a table. Let me take your coat.' He caught it as it dropped from her shoulders, and hung it on the stand under the stairs. They walked towards the corner table where the waiter had pulled out a chair for her.

'So how has your week been?' he asked.

'Long. I seem to be wading through beaurocracy at the moment.'

'Sounds fun.' He smiled and pulled out a cigarette. 'Do you mind?'

'No, it's fine. The work is just tedious sometimes and you wonder really how it helps, if at all.'

'Jana, it's important.

'I know, you're right. It's just that I wonder if it makes a difference with me being there.'

'Of course it does. Just because you want to make a difference in life it doesn't mean you need to have a job that no one else does.'

She felt annoyed by his assumptions, and even more irritated that he felt he could just order wine without consulting her.

'Our best red, sir,' the waiter declared, showing Lukas the bottle.

He nodded, and the waiter poured it into her glass before she could comment. When both glasses were filled, Lukas lifted his and clinked it against her glass with enough clout to raise the eyebrows of the lone man sitting smoking his pipe on the table next to theirs.

'*Na zdraví*,' they both chimed.

Jana took a sip of the wine. It was mellow and fruity, and it slid down pleasantly. Friday, what a great day of the week. She put the glass down and played with the stem.

'Enough about me making a difference, how was your week?'

'Oh, same things really,' he said looking her up and down as though it was their first meeting.

'Have you had your hair done?'

'Yes, Monday. Very observant.'

'I like it. Very cute.' She rolled the ends through her fingers. Their conversation was stopped momentarily by the jazz band warming up by the bar. The saxophonist started to flow through notes like a butterfly flitting from one flower to the next, and the trumpet player pulled items out of his case like a well-rehearsed magician.

The third, a rotund man, set up the keyboard and collected drinks from the bar. The room was already smoke-filled, adding to the atmosphere of the small tavern. It felt more like someone's home than a city restaurant. The owner was a lively man who greeted the customers and mingled with them, listening to the music. He had a penchant for jazz and, according to rumours, used to play with the band many years ago.

The man at the neighbouring table looked up from his paper long enough to watch the warm-up and take a swig of beer from his glass. One couple was talking intensely on the table by the window, and a group of older women at the adjacent table were laughing.

'So how's the castle project going?' Jana put her glass down and picked up the menu.

'Good. I think. It's early days, but the press meeting went well, I think.

'They seem to be taking an interest in your work. It's

impressive.'

'It's an important part of the history of the castle. The mosaic is one of a kind.'

Jana nodded and gazed across at the ladies, now ploughing through bottles of white wine and laughing, their bodies shaking and their arms waving in the air. She envied their ease of conversation and glanced back at Lukas, wondering if there was any chance of something more. It had been months since she had kissed him and, although they had been tactile, he was distant and preoccupied.

She watched the curls falling across his forehead. At times throughout the evening she felt as though she was an outsider looking in through a murky window frame.

Lukas was so involved in his work, so elusive and intriguing. As much as she tried to resist her thoughts, there was something compelling about his dedication to the project. Momentary shadows of remembrance would appear across his face and then leave just as quickly. She struggled to see what was behind his expressions. He was unique and puzzling. In truth, she was missing some of his conversation as she studied the details of his face.

'I try to imagine the mosaic in its restored state' said Lukas.

'Yes, I've seen pictures of the original,' she said. 'It's a powerful image.'

An almost invisible dimple on his cheek would appear just as he was trying to describe a detail. The corners of his lips would curl, and it just appeared. His eyes sparkled beyond the candlelight, lighting up as he spoke about something that inspired him.

'Have you seen much of Benes recently?' she asked.

He shook his head. 'No, why?'

'I haven't seen my sister this week. It's hard to find time with her. I miss her,'

'Irena?'

'Yes, we used to see so much of each other and now life seems to be absorbing all our time. I've been busy with work and she's married. It's just that I can't help feeling that I'm losing her.'

Lukas looked at her quizzically. His eyes wandered as if trying to recall something and then, there it was again, the shadow across his face. He looked pained.

'Are you OK?' she asked.

'Yes, fine. Did you see each other much before they got married?'

'We often spoke on the phone when I was in Letovice, and when I came home we spent time together organising her wedding. We were close growing up, there were no secrets between us. I don't believe that anything should be hidden.'

'I still see Benes,' he said. He looked awkward. 'We meet for drinks.'

'Irena sometimes calls when he's out with you. They seem happy, don't you think?'

'Yes, they're a good combination.'

'She's always been quite independent,' said Jana.

'And what do you want from life?' Lukas asked.

He asked the question if he was just offering another glass

of wine. He leaned in towards the table, glass in hand, and shirt collar slightly ruffled. Jana pushed the dumplings around her plate and stared into the candle as if it would provide the answer. The music stopped momentarily, and the chatter continued on the surrounding tables. The waiter appeared and refilled their water glasses, then checked that the food was to their liking.

'*Perfektní, děkuji*, thank you,' said Lukas, his voice soft and familiar.

She hung on to his last 'thank you.' The smoke-filled room made him look like a portrait painting she had seen as a girl.

'I just want to find purpose in what I do, and to discover new things. I don't need security because I've learned that no one can give you that. At least, it's wrong to expect it.'

He watched her intently – it was unnerving – then stretched his arm across the table to stroke her cheek.

'Jana, you're a fighter, I can't imagine you'd ever rely on someone else. You look as though you don't need anyone at all.'

He took her glass away and kissed her. She pulled back, brushing her hair away from her face.

'What was that?'

'What do you mean?'

'Well, when I kissed you in the park you practically ran away.' She had finally found the courage to say it to him.

'I know, I've regretted it ever since.'

'I assumed you weren't interested,' she said quietly, hoping he wouldn't hear her above the saxophonist.

'I'm sorry, Jana. It took me by surprise, and then we were both busy. I thought it had just become a friendship. I didn't dare push it. I've wanted to kiss you. It's just been difficult to know how to play it,' he continued.

'Play?' she said, indignantly. 'I'm not going to play games with you, Lukas. I like you but I won't be messed around. I want us to be straight with each other.'

She knew a relationship needed an element of mystery but she was resistant to any more emotional turmoil. The sense of loss in her life was too great to risk any further pain. Her life was running smoothly and on the surface, at least, she was fine.

'I didn't mean it like that,' he protested. 'I just didn't know what you wanted. The night you rang, when I was preparing for the press conference, I wanted to ask you to come over, but I couldn't. I didn't want to presume anything.'

The band rattled a bluesy rendition of her favourite jazz music, and the elderly man at the table across the room filled his pipe with more tobacco, stuffing it in like cushion filling. The room was thick with smoke, obscuring the animated faces. The atmosphere was jovial, celebratory almost. The owner had taken over the drums while the original drummer sat at the bar talking to some of the other locals.

The ladies at the table across from them had consumed too many bottles to count and looked flushed. The conversations were exuberant, unlike that of the couple beneath the window, who now spoke in low whispers over a dessert of some fancy cake with cream.

She looked again at Lukas. 'Life's too short to worry about offending people or waiting to see what happens. There are so many things I wanted to tell my father that I wish I had done. You never know what's next, so you have to seize the moment. I think that's why I kissed you when we were by the fountain, but it backfired.'

'I'm sorry,' he said. 'Can we take it from here?'

'Here being?'

He took a gulp of wine and filled both of their glasses, the liquid sloshed against the insides and slid down into a pool of deep burgundy. 'I don't know really, I suppose I just want to start again.'

Jana raised her glass in a toast. 'To new beginnings.'

'To new beginnings,' he echoed faintly.

Chapter 21

'Morning.' Katerina stood at the door. 'Lunch at one?'

'Yes. That would be great,' said Jana, 'good weekend?'

'Visited family. I'll fill you in later.'

She turned on her needlepoint heels and trotted down the corridor. Pavel didn't arrive until half past nine and Jana relished that half-hour just to sort through the things on her desk and acclimatise to the needs of the day. She usually began with a strong coffee and opened the window to let some fresh air into the room. There was nothing like a good espresso – sharp, intense, and steaming hot. The scent of warm, ground coffee beans revived her mind. It was difficult to get Lukas out of her head.

She hadn't planned to go back to his apartment, they had just ended up on his doorstep. She couldn't really remember. He had said something about showing her some photographs of the castle mosaic. In her alcohol-induced state she had smiled and allowed him to lead her by the hand.

It was yesterday morning – when she awoke to the sound of the trams passing by under the open window of his apartment – that she remembered she wasn't at home. She rolled over to see his dark curls and his arm stretched across the blanket towards her. His eyes flickered slowly, dreaming, somewhere miles away.

She slid out of the bed, careful not to wake him, and could hear his light breathing as she edged towards the kitchen. Jana put the kettle on the gas flame of the hob and wandered back across the living room to his bookshelves. They were full of journals and archaeological books. To her surprise, the lower shelves were full of political books and articles.

Some of the spines were illegible, unless she squinted or moved closer. They looked well used, reminding her of her father's collection. He hadn't mentioned that he was interested in politics. She was drawn in by the array of books on the economic and social systems. The kettle hissed, threatening to burst with volcanic steam.

Finding two clean mugs in the cupboard, she placed them on the work surface and spooned coffee into each one. The oven could do with a good clean. It was probably the last thing on his mind after a day's work. He had a scruffy efficiency about him and he looked dishevelled but he never missed a detail or a date. She glanced back at his sleeping body, his chest rising and falling peacefully. It was the first time she had seen him look peaceful. His restlessness pervaded his character and his words and conversations. It was difficult to put a finger on what was wrong. He acted as though he were a fugitive.

She discarded the thought and looked aimlessly out of the window and watched the lady opposite hanging out her washing. Red roof tiles and washing lines spread out into the distance in a sea of clay and fabrics. Jana found the biscuits next to the tea bags and munched on one slowly, savouring the taste of almond. A half-empty milk carton sat abandoned in the fridge and she sniffed it to see if it was still useable. It smelled fresh enough.

Lukas stirred and rolled away from her line of vision. He buried his head under the pillow like a dog. The light caught the curves of his back. She felt a tingle of excitement. It had all happened so quickly. She took the opportunity to look around the apartment. Picking up her mug and another biscuit, she wandered out of the kitchen and into the living room. There was not much to look at until she glanced up towards a shelf in the corner of the room. A shiny ornament caught her eye and then a small, old and worn photo of a woman, possibly his mother, looking shyly at the camera. Where was his father? Remembering their conversation at the cemetery about his grandparents she felt a sense of grief sweep over her. It must have been harrowing for his mother to lose them in the camp.

The coffee was warm and comforting and she could smell breakfast filtering up from the apartment below. It was strange being in someone else's apartment like this. She looked down at the old t-shirt she had thrown on. Jana had found it lying

192

over the chair and it swamped her.

Catching a glimpse of herself in the mirror, she could see mascara smudged under her eyes, and made her way to the bathroom, splashed her face with cold water, and patted it with the small brown towel on the rail.

She walked back to the bookshelf out of some kind of compulsion. In much the same way that iron filings are drawn to a magnet, something forced her to look again. Books that had become worn at the edges sat in a heap on the shelf. *Sorry*, *The Garden Party*, *Temptation*, *The Mistake*. These were all plays by Havel. She recognised them because her father had copies of every play he had written to date. These looked well read and cherished.

Jana pulled out the book in the middle entitled *Memorandum*, and a small notebook came with it, tumbling down on to the rug beneath her bare feet. Battered and worn, it looked like a journal or a diary of some sort. Sitting on the sofa, with the notebook in one hand and the mug in the other, she leaned forward to see if Lukas was still sleeping. From the living room she had a clear view through the bedroom door which was slightly open.

As she began to read the words on the pages in front of her, a sense of apprehension rose from her gut. Her pulse quickened. Names, scattered across the pages, notes on their whereabouts, personal information – all scrawled, in hast, onto the paper. The author was in a rush, pressured. Rifling through pages, she was unable to decipher the information. Why would you keep notes on people like this? Chillingly, her father's name leapt up from the page.

'Radek Maček:

Wife, daughters – Jana and Irena. Son, Aleš.

Working against the state.

Lectures given on Economic Freedom, Democracy and Governance.'

How could he have known her father? Taking a last gulp of coffee, as if she would never taste it again, she looked at the notebook in shock. Why was he taking notes on her father? Had he been on their side, working for the secret police? How? Her heart was pounding, her stomach threatened to drive up into her throat. Tatínek, turned in by the man she had just spent the night with? The man she thought she loved? She shuddered.

How could he do this to Tatínek? He was a good man, a kind man. 'Tatínek!' Jana shouted his name in her mind. She wanted to shout it out loud. What if the informer woke up? Her mind raced at a speed she could hardly follow. She felt faint and gripped with fear. The blood coursed through her veins, her hands shook and her chest tightened.

She trusted him. At least she thought she did. Looking up into the bedroom she could see his hand draped over the side of the bed. He had rolled over and was lying on his back, deep in sleep.

In the moments that passed and, as the questions stormed through her mind, what Jana couldn't understand was how a conservator had ended up in this position. Weren't they meant to do just that – conserve? She knew there must have been a reason why he had turned, but why her family, and how had they now found each other? Had he tracked her down?

She felt cold.

Sitting in silence, Jana picked up the notebook to discover more murky information. There was nothing which made any sense to her, and names which she had never heard of. Some were code words and much of his scribbling was indecipherable.

So this was what they wanted. It was as if a light had been switched on. All these years of never knowing what happened and now she was presented with first-hand evidence. She felt like a juror, about to pass some kind of sentence, but the irony was that her father had already served his sentence and lost his life as a result.

They had been told when he was released from prison that the pneumonia, caught whilst inside, had weakened his system and he was likely to catch more infections. 'It's not uncommon,' she remembered the doctor saying. Jana pictured the moment when she had stood in the kitchen of their apartment as a child. Dr Rusek looked into her eyes and, perhaps seeing her fear rising, reassured her that he was all right for now. For now – what did that mean? She knew he was slowly getting weaker, but to what extent, no one could tell.

The door opened, and she was jolted back toreality.

'Shall we eat?' Katerina asked as she swirled into the room.

'What time is it?' Jana looked at the large clock on the wall. 'Is it that time already? Yes, let's go.'

'Are you all right? You look distracted. Shall I come back later?'

'No, no, it's all right,' Jana insisted.

The canteen bustled with life as they picked up a tray each. She didn't feel hungry, the dumpling soup and a small roll would be enough. Her stomach had been churning all morning and she hadn't been able to sleep or eat properly.

They found a space in the corner of the canteen in the sunlight and Katerina put down her tray of meat, vegetables and some kind of glazed cake, and went in search of the water jug. She poured two glasses and sat down looking Jana squarely in the face, as if she was analysing a patient.

'So how was the weekend?' She handed Jana the glass of water and dived into the food. 'I'm hungry, tell me everything and then I'll fill you in on mine as soon as my stomach stops growling.'

Jana didn't know where to begin. Not wanting to open up a whole story on which she couldn't close the lid, she answered vaguely.

'I did some housework for Matka and caught up with friends. You?'

'What about Miloš?' Katerina asked. 'Have you heard from him?'

She'd forgotten how much she had talked about him in the early weeks of the new job, and had tried to push him to the back of her mind, along with the rest of the clutter that she couldn't deal with at the time.

'I haven't really heard from him. I don't expect to. He's busy with the community projects and I haven't contacted him much myself. We write from time to time.'

Her time in Letovice felt a million miles away and so, too, did Miloš. They couldn't be together so she had to be pragmatic about it and move on for now. Pragmatism was something that Tatínek had taught her. It was an essential life skill.

Katerina looked concerned. 'Are you all right? I know I asked you earlier, but really, are you OK? You look pale and you're too quiet. You're never quiet at lunchtime. Come on.'

'I saw Lukas this weekend.'

'Why didn't you say?'

'It's no big thing really.' Jana swept her hair back and knotted it into the nape of her neck, looking up at Katerina. It was a big thing.

'Yes, and?'

'Well, I stayed the night.'

'OK. More information please.'

Katerina teased it out of her like a trainer coaxing a horse over a jump.

'It was great. No, terrible, actually.'

Katerina frowned and dropped her fork, which destroyed the decoration of the pink dessert on her plate.

'Have I missed a bit somewhere?'

'He was great company and the night kind of rolled on into

the morning, but then I wandered around his apartment...'

'What were you doing going through his things? You stayed the night?'

'Wait, let me finish. I wasn't going through his things, I was just looking around and I found a notebook on his bookshelf. It wasn't exactly tucked away.'

Pavel wandered past and nodded in their direction. He must have seen from the expressions on their faces that now was not a time to interrupt the conversation.

'What do you mean? Was it just sitting with the other books?' Katerina gulped her water down and played with the pieces of cake left on her plate.

'Yes, I skimmed through it and maybe I shouldn't have. No, I had every right to see, I saw names. There were names everywhere, including mine, Irena's, Aleš's, Matka's, Tatínek's. Kat, it was awful.' She started to choke.

'I'm confused. Why would he write about your family? How would he even know?' She stopped mid-sentence, almost with bitter recognition. 'Don't tell me, you think he was an informer? Do you?'

'Well, what would you think?'

'What did you say to him?'

'I didn't, I'm a coward. I just got dressed and left.'

Katerina tilted her head to one side and looked at Jana with an expression that beckoned more information.

'You just left?'

Jana was beginning to feel exasperated. 'I just left. I don't know. What was I supposed to do? I panicked, and I haven't spoken to him since, or heard from him.'

'Did you put the book back?'

'Of course.' This was beginning to feel like a cross-examination.

'Katerina, I really don't know what to do. He probably thinks I just panicked about staying and left to avoid too much conversation.'

'Let's hope so.'

'What do you mean?'

'I just hope he didn't know you found it, the notebook. What will you do?'

Jana looked at Katerina and she felt a sense of panic. 'I don't know. I haven't slept. I've been trying to figure out why. It's not exactly every day you discover you're dating the person who had your father imprisoned. Katerina, my father wouldn't have died if he...' Tears filled her eyes and she wrestled to form the rest of the sentence, 'If he hadn't been kept inside for so long. It tore families apart. We survived, but only just.'

Chapter 22

Katerina marched into Jana's office with a collection files.

'I found his name.'

'Whose name?'

'Lukas. Who did you think?'

'Is this legitimate?' She felt flustered.

'Jana, we need to get to the bottom of this.' She dropped the files and took a step back from the desk.

'What did you find out?'

'Have a look.' Katerina leaned forward and pulled out the thickest file. 'Here, look at this one.'

Jana felt her stomach lurch as she tentatively leafed through the pages.

'LUKAS JOSIAH DOBRANSKY.'

The words shouted at her from the top of the first page. She closed the file and picked up her coffee.

'What are you doing?' Katerina asked. 'Don't you want to know? If it were me ...'

Jana stopped her in her tracks. 'Well you're not.'

'I just think you should look. It won't kill you.'

She felt the defiance rising in her. She braced herself and tried to respond calmly. Why did she need to use the word 'kill'?

'Look, I just need some time, that's all. It's still a shock and I don't know if I'm ready to find out the whole truth just yet.'

'I understand that, but at some point you need to know. It's better to find out now.'

Jana pulled a chair across the room from Pavel's desk and beckoned her accomplice to sit down. An accomplice was just how she saw her at this moment. They were about to hack into a secret life. The files were now open and information could be disclosed legally, but it didn't mean she was ready.

'Why haven't you looked before?' asked Katerina. 'For your father's records.'

'I didn't think there was any more to find out. He told me everything as far as I know, so why should I feel the need to delve deeper? That would suggest I didn't take him at his word.'

'But now there's Lukas,' said Katerina.

'I know. I've been thinking all afternoon, trying to work out if there was a connection that my father would have known about.'

'And what have you come up with?'

'*Nic*, nothing. All I can see, when I close my eyes, are the words in Lukas's notebook. If I hadn't found it, I'd be living with a lie. I don't understand how he could see me, knowing what he'd done, unless he was unaware of the link.'

'That's what I was hoping too,' said Katerina. 'How would anyone be able to live with that kind of knowledge, and hide it so well from someone they cared for?'

Katerina put the rest of the papers down and sat beside her. Jana gathered her thoughts. Maybe this hadn't been such a good idea. Re-opening the file, she leafed through the pages starting at the beginning. It gave all of his qualifications and stated his profession. There was some information on his family and his place of birth.

'No living parents'.

'No parents.' She repeated the words aloud, feeling like a criminal investigator. Jana glanced warily at Katerina.

'It's OK. You need to know,' said Katerina.

'He talked about his mother but not his father. She survived a concentration camp but lost her brother, from what I know.'

As she read through the file the words started to jump around, and she could feel her heart pounding. It felt as though it was going to rip through her chest. She could feel her body tighten as she gripped the folder. The words made her feel weak.

'Do you want me to read it to you?' asked Katerina.

'No, it's OK. I just don't know what I'll do once I've finished with all of this.'

Katerina put her hand on Jana's arm, as if to steady her.

'Keep reading. It's the only way you can move forward now.'

'What do you mean?'

'I just think you have to find out, that's all. Don't think that everything will explode in front of you. It's in the past, so whatever you see in the next few minutes can't be undone.'

'I don't understand why he didn't tell me.' She took a deep breath.

'Jana, you're strong and you like him, don't you?'

'But this changes everything, don't you see? Part of me doesn't want to know. I know that might sound strange to you, but I want to pretend this never happened.'

'You have to know. You said yourself, you might have been living a lie if you hadn't discovered the notebook. Don't you want to know the whole truth?'

Jana looked at her for a moment, then turned towards the window. 'My father might have lived if he hadn't been imprisoned for so long. He might still be alive.'

Katerina leaned forwards and opened the file, letting the front cover drop down on the desk. She got up and walked towards the door. She left quietly.

Jana didn't know whether to be angry with Lukas or with the whole system. She knew, at some deeper level, that there must have been some sense of desperation on his part to force him into this kind of deceit. She knew enough to realise that the forces that her father had been fighting against for so long were dark and coercive at best, and at worst they ate away the very core of a person's soul.

She learned over the minutes that followed that Lukas, although not responsible for the initial imprisonment of her father, had been the one to keep him there – a captivity so extreme that it drove many to suicide. Tatínek had never told her, but she knew. She knew more than he ever realised. Had he been released sooner, as she suspected, he might not have died of pneumonia. Did it make Lukas a killer? A murderer? How could he look her in the eyes, knowing the truth? The relationship was a lie.

Feelings of betrayal rose up within her, threatening to strangle any hope of moving forward. The word 'truth' resounded in her mind. Katerina was right, she had to weed out the lies and find the facts. Jana could see, from months of reading the files, that people were trapped in so many ways. No one was free. A cocoon of lies had encased individuals within the workings of a dark underworld. The question was, who and why? If she could see Lukas as a hostage, maybe it would help her to understand.

Was this really all that was left behind? Words on pieces of paper, notebooks, photographs?

Chapter 23

'I'm at a loss as to what to do, Irena,' said Jana. The sun lowered over the city's horizon as they walked along the river. 'Thank you for coming to meet me, I know you've been busy. I miss you.'

Her sister put a gentle arm around her, and for a moment Jana felt fine. The revelations of the day were temporarily washed away. Deep down, though, she knew that some things would have to be resolved. It felt that every time she jumped over a hurdle there was a boulder in the way, and this one wasn't going to shift quickly.

'If only we could rewind to our younger days, Rei.'

'Have you confronted him? Have you asked him what actually happened? All you have is the file and the notebooks. You need to find out the truth. It was a cruel time, and few people knew what really happened behind the walls of people's houses or a prison cell. Sometimes men and women were forced into doing awful things.'

Jana disliked her sister's stark, practical advice. It made sense, but it negated her pain. She fought back the tear that was threatening to bring more with it. 'I just don't understand how, how.' Her words tailed off. Irena turned towards her.

'What?' she asked gently.

'I can't bring myself to face him. I don't understand how he could face me, knowing what he did.'

'I can understand your anger and we all feel the same betrayal but you don't know what he was put through, Jana. You don't know his story. Ask him before you jump to conclusions.'

Jana thought she knew him, but everyone had a story and she was beginning to acknowledge that she had only gleaned the surface of his story. Her mind leapt back to the morning when she woke in his apartment. How little she knew in the moments before the discovery. He looked beautiful and so peaceful, lying in the morning light. She found him fascinating.

'I'm not telling you to just accept it, but don't be too harsh in your judgement of him, at least not until you know the facts.'

Jana hated unpredictability in life. How could Irena put it so simply? Her sister was so precise. It made her a good lawyer, but it was faintly frustrating. Giving someone the benefit of the doubt would erase the grounds for her anger. She had to fit the pieces together to find the full picture, gather the evidence herself. Jana's mind flashed back to Lukas's description of the mosaic. He had explained to her that the full picture was often misrepresented if all of the tiles were not carefully excavated.

'Jana? Did you hear what I said?'

'Hmm? Yes, sorry, I was just thinking. I was wondering what it would be like to put him on trial.'

'But you don't know the truth,' said Irena. 'What I mean is, you can't just decide he's guilty. We're not in court. This is life, your life, his life. Speak to him.'

She felt like a small, insignificant piece of a much larger puzzle. The colours of the sky now reflected deep reds. It should be a beautiful day tomorrow.

'I can't, what are you supposed to say? I don't know what the truth is and I don't know how to approach him or how he'll react. In a way it's easier not knowing.'

'But you can't live like that.' She knew her sister was right.

'Jana,' Irena continued, 'you once told me to face facts and move forward. You said there was no point in worrying about the 'could-have-beens' or 'might-bes.' Now I'm going to ask you to do just that.'

Jana rolled her eyes upwards towards the sky as if waiting for some sort of inspiration. She wondered for a moment if she could just pretend nothing had happened. Hadn't there been enough pain already? As if reading her mind, Irena asked her another question.

'Don't hide from problems, don't bury this with no conclusion. What would Tatínek have said to you?'

The thought made her freeze. Her life looked so small in comparison to what Tatínek had achieved.

'I spoke to Matka.'

'Yes?' said Irena. 'What did she say?'

'Well, she was shocked and upset but she also said that I had to work out what I wanted from this, from Lukas and from what I discovered. She asked me if I loved him and if it was worth throwing it all away for a ghost.'

'What do you mean?' Irena asked. They both knew Matka always got straight to the point.

'I think she meant I couldn't hang on to Tatínek or the pain of his loss, or the revelations. She's so pragmatic. It's almost as though she has no grief.'

Irena was silent for a while. Fiddling with her gold bracelet. Jana waited. The air felt thicker, as it did at this time of year, and the cars moved slowly in the distance across the bridge. Maybe people heading home from work for the weekend to see their families, maybe people heading out of the city. Who knew where they were going?

'She must have been shocked to hear about Lukas. I'm sure she's grieving in her own way, Jana. Matka just has to move on and maybe she wants to see you happy. She wants you to be free of all this.'

It was frustrating when other people formed opinions of her, especially when they didn't really know her mind. Everybody had an opinion on her job and her current situation, but nobody could solve or erase the pain.

She felt bolted to the ground while others carried on with

their lives, as though nothing had ever been wrong. Maybe it was time to confront Lukas if she was going to break free. He was a key into the past and, despite all the damage done, he might be able to offer her something, a glimpse into the past.

'Jana. My notebook. How could you read it? I didn't expect you to go riffling through my belongings.' Lukas paced across the floor, heading towards the kitchen. His apartment was tidier now. It looked as though he had cleared things away. She followed him like a lamb. As they stood motionless she examined the pottery mugs on the shelf and remembered that morning – the light streaming in through the window, the smell of the room.

How had she managed to keep the contents of the notebook to herself? Why hadn't she confronted him earlier? The new findings in the government vaults had given her fresh ammunition, as if the notebook alone hadn't been enough. Maybe she had needed the time to consider, to build up to this, and think through what she would say. Honestly, she hadn't any idea what to say.

'I didn't mean to, it just fell out and I was curious.' His anger stifled her feelings and all the words that she had planned to say.

'Curious,' said Lukas abruptly. 'Just plain nosey.'

'Lukas, I refuse to apologise and I demand an explanation. You owe me that.'

'I owe you nothing.' His tone had changed and his demeanour was now defensive. This felt like some kind of animalistic head-to-head combat. They were both determined and sitting on some degree of anger, which was threatening to explode in front of them.

'I owe you nothing,' he repeated. The volume of his voice dropped and he turned towards the kitchen window.

'Lukas, I refuse to let you fob me off. I deserve to know the truth.'

'Jana, you don't understand what you're getting into here. I can't begin to explain the things that went on.'

How differently she had felt the last time she saw him here. She couldn't bear to lose him, neither did she wish to hear the truth. She didn't know how extreme his anger would become and was beginning to see a side of him which was cold and disconnected. Jana tried to imagine how he could have felt while he was imprisoned, but it was impossible. He now felt like a stranger to her, with a history she couldn't reach or understand. She couldn't touch his pain, his anger, his disappointment. Something inside her felt desperate. She grabbed his arms and turned him towards her.

'Please,' she pleaded with him, 'just tell me. I thought about living without knowing, but I can't. Just tell me something, anything. What about Tatínek?'

His face crumpled, he refused to look at her.

'I can't, Jana. I can't.'

'You have to. I can't live with half-truths. Lukas, I have your file.' His head raised with a jolt.

'My file? I don't understand. What file?'

'Your records, government records. I know they don't tell

the whole truth, so now you'll have to fill me in.'

'What do they say?' He had an animal-in-headlights look that told her he wanted to bolt.

'I can't share that with you, it's classified information, but I know that you knew him.'

'I'm a traitor, Jana. I had no idea when I met you who you were. When I found out who your father was I was racked with guilt, but I couldn't hurt you and I couldn't leave. Night after night I've replayed everything in my mind, and then I see your face in all its sweetness and innocence and it makes me shake and sweat. Don't think I'm not constantly haunted by this.'

'I'm not a child.' She was indignant. 'You don't have to water this down for me.'

'I know, but I've corrupted something so good.'

'Stop. Stop this. I'm not good, I'm angry. I won't stop until I get the facts so you have all the time in the world, starting now. It's up to you, Lukas.'

She took a step back. He lowered his head and ran his hands through his hair. He did the same thing when he was upset or recalling details.

'I think I knew when we were at the fountain,' he said. 'Something stopped me kissing you. I couldn't work out what, but when I found out who you were I knew why I felt so uncomfortable. That's why I pulled away when you kissed me. Something told me not to, but I wanted it. You look much so like him, Jana.'

As Lukas continued, she walked slowly into the living room and collapsed on the sofa. This time he followed her. She began to fade out his justifications and explanations, slipping back into a time when her father was alive. She remembered when they watched the television and the news of the Berlin Wall being destroyed, recalling feelings of fear of the impending political changes in their country. Changes her father had been ranting about, and ones which were now a reality.

How had a country with close-knit families and a rich culture reached such a state of distrust? It had been torn apart by so many lies. The changes were monumental and they mirrored the stages of her journey with the man she had grown to both love and hate.

Her lack of trust in him was now only because of the truth. Why was it that deep down she wished she didn't know the reality of what had happened? Is it better not to know, to live with a lie and have no knowledge of the reality? The questions poured through her mind like a torrent of water travelling towards the ocean, picking up boulders along the way.

How could he have lived with all this for so long? Wasn't the truth, as Tatínek had said, supposed to set you free? This wasn't freedom in any shape or form. They were both trapped. He stood towering over her as she sat slumped on the sofa. He was menacing, and his physical height above her was intimidating.

'Why did you wait to tell me you knew?' he insisted. 'Answer me that.'

'You're asking me why I waited? Are you going to accuse me of a delay when you've held all this without telling me?'

'It's different,' said Lukas. 'I mean you can't compare it.'

'And how might that be?' Jana demanded an answer. She stood up to face him, and although he was still taller than her she felt a renewed strength sweep through her mind.

'Lukas, my father died and he might have lived if it hadn't been for you, for your selfish, foolish decisions. And don't tell me I don't understand. I do, Lukas, I do.'

She walked towards the window and waited for his response. Facing him was too intense. Standing with her back towards him was an act of defiance, and it shielded her so that her expressions were masked. Only the people on the street below could see her now. Most of them didn't ever look up, so she was safe. A man with a dark umbrella twirled it slightly as he walked. A young girl held someone's hand and a dog ran ahead. The street looked otherwise quiet.

She wished she could just wash this away and go back to the oblivion of the untruths, the unknowns and the questions that had been much less complicated than this.

Lukas moved towards her and tentatively placed his hand on her shoulder.

'Jana, I can't presume to really know you, to understand what you went through when you lost him, or even how you felt when the truth unraveled, but I do know that you need to bury the past. I know that I've fuelled your pain and for that I'm deeply sorry.'

'For that?' she replied. 'What about what happened inside? You betrayed him, Lukas. You kept him there and now he's gone. How can you live with yourself? How can you...' Her

213

words trailed off into the distance. Tears began to roll down her cheeks, her shoulders hunched and her body started to coil. Slowly he turned her around to face him.

'I'm not proud of myself, Jana. You have to understand the extreme situation we were in. People were inside for no reason, no reason. The man in the cell next door had been arrested because his neighbour had had a disagreement with him. The neighbour didn't like him, and framed him for activities he hadn't even engaged in. Some were sent to labour camps, or executed. It was a living hell. I had to get out, and it was the only way I could secure my freedom.'

She was enraged. 'Your freedom? Your freedom cost lives, many of them, Lukas. I saw from the files that it wasn't just my father you incriminated, there were more. Innocent men, and most of them died inside.' His face dropped.

'The files must be detailed. I try not to remember most of it. Is there much point in thrashing all this out? It won't bring them back. I can't undo this, Jana. I can't keep reliving it either.'

She felt sick. The thought of Tatínek trusting this man was awful. Tatínek was a good man, he was honest.

'Jana, I know I've harmed you, harmed your family. You'll never know the depths of the system. It leaves you trapped in a web of deceit. When I say trapped, I mean caught, against my will at every turn. It's a torment that I would never wish on anyone. But I had to have hope, hope for change, and for freedom.'

Chapter 24

'Jana?' came the voice from the end of the line.

'Speaking,' she said. Jana hadn't heard his voice for some time. She shook slightly when she heard his words.

'I miss you.'

'Miloš?' she said, struggling to find a response. She knew his voice. 'How are you?' So many thoughts flooded her mind that it was hard to hear what he was saying to her.

'I started medical school, and it's great so far. A lot of work, but it's no more than I expected.'

'That's great, Miloš. So you're here, in Prague?'

'Yes, I got into Charles University. I'm here in the city, your city.'

'Lukas, that's amazing.'

'Miloš,' he corrected her. 'It's Miloš!' She caught her breath, wishing she could swallow the words.

'Who is Lukas?'

'He's a friend, Miloš. I'm tired, I'm sorry. Do you want to meet up? Shall we catch up properly?' She tried to avoid a long conversation and any further slips.

'Great, I'll come over and pick you up. Tomorrow night? I have your address, don't I?'

'What time?

'Is seven OK for you?' '

'Yes, see you then.'

Her hand shook as she put the receiver down. Missing the base, it slipped and fell on to the floor, bouncing, as if trying to escape her grip. How had she got his name wrong? A better question was why hadn't she realised that he would be going to Charles University? They had four faculties: Theology, Arts, Law and Medicine. He always said he could switch if he changed his mind. He would be following in the footsteps of the likes of Franz Kafka.

'Jana?' Matka shouted from the bathroom, 'Who was that? Was it for me?' Matka said she would be expecting a call from a friend.

'No, Matka, it was for me.' She watched her mother gathering up the washing.

'Who was it? Lukas?' Jana wasn't ready for more questions. 'Are you all right, my love? You look flushed.'

Matka looked worried. She stroked Jana's cheeks and frowned.

'It's all right,' she continued, 'you don't have to tell me, I was just checking you're OK, that's all.'

'Actually it was Miloš.'

'Ah.' Something in her expression told Jana that she already knew.

'And how is he? Is he studying? He's a nice boy.'

Jana was startled by Matka's comment. 'You haven't met him. How do you know if he's nice?'

'He came over one afternoon when you were at work.'

'Why would he do that? When?' She steadied herself against the table.

'A week or so ago, I don't remember, but I liked him – smart, interesting, warm.'

Why didn't you tell me? Did he have a message?'

Matka looked down. 'I made a mess of things. I called him Lukas. I'm sorry, I don't think he took kindly to it and I had to explain. I told him you were friends.' She clutched a towel, pressed it into her stomach, and breathed out slowly. 'Why are you smiling, girl?'

'Ah, Matka, I made the same mistake on the phone.' They both laughed.

'You know, Jana, you don't have to do what you think people expect of you all the time. It's OK to follow your heart.' There was a long, lingering silence as they studied each other. 'The question is, do you know what your heart is telling you?'

Matka folded the towels, picking each one up from the heap in the basket. She looked quizzically at Jana.

'Matka, I don't know, I really don't know,' she said, glancing at the crumpled pile of washing.

Well, you've seen a fair amount of that Lukas character in recent months.'

Matka's statement reminded Jana that she hadn't really met Lukas properly. Maybe he had deliberately kept away. Seeing her mother, a widow, should induce feelings of guilt if he had any form of a conscience.

'I tried to close the door with Miloš. I didn't think I'd hear from him again. His career is important to him and he was abroad for so long. You know, Matka, when people are that focused on what they're doing it's hard to find a gap in their lives. You feel that you'll never be an important part of their plans.'

'Jana, you're made of sterner material than that. Are you just going to give up because, as you say, he's been busy? Do you love him?' She didn't know how to respond to Matka's directness. 'Let me put it this way, who would you think of if you couldn't see either of them again? Who do you trust?'

Trust was overrated, and she was beginning to distrust everything, even her own judgement.

'All I know,' said Jana, 'is that life gets confusing sometimes. It throws things at you sideways that you can't or don't expect.'

'Jana, there's hope in any situation. It's how your father kept going in the difficult times.'

The thought of Tatínek and his difficulties made her feel anxious. If only things were that simple. She was at a time in her life when she was supposed to be having fun.. It was endearing, the way her mother showed concern, and she normally loved her for her frankness.

'You know,' said Jana, 'It'll be OK. Everything will be OK, you'll see.' She wasn't sure if she was trying to reassure Matka or herself, but for the moment it helped her to think that way. It gave her some kind of peace of mind and some degree of hope that things would smooth out, and that she would find the right path to take, the right plan of action. She needed a plan.

Jana helped Matka to fold the last few pieces and took them to her room, passing the statue of the couple on the table to the side of the hallway. It had been there for as long as she could remember. As a young girl, it had encapsulated for her the idea of closeness and trust. The way the arms of the couple entwined around each other looked safe, but it was an illusion. Life wasn't safe, it was a series of events that needed to be tackled, resisted or surmounted.

Jana put the washing down and sat on her bed with a book, one of many novels she had recently devoured. It helped to take her mind off her thoughts, and provided the escape that she needed.

Chapter 25

As they sat by the side of the river Jana watched the reflections dance in the evening light. The city felt strangely quiet, and the usual buzz and bustle of people and cars were silenced this evening. '*Shon*' was what Tatínek always said of the city, 'bustle' – that frantic mix of noise and movement, which mirrored her turmoil.

She listened to Miloš talk about his experiences in the Philippines and wondered how it had changed him. Every new situation had to change a person, she thought, it had to change the way they saw the world and the way they processed ideas.

They had only been together for a few hours, and already she felt the ease of being with him. It was as if no time had passed since leaving Letovice. He had changed, he was grittier, tougher, more self-assured. There was a tone in his voice that sounded new and stronger. He hadn't lost his warmth or his enthusiasm. She loved him for those qualities, but dare not admit it to herself.

'Jana, I've missed you.'

He grasped her hand carefully. His movements were smoother than Lukas's sudden reflex responses.

Miloš continued to talk. 'Did you miss me? I didn't hear from you towards the end.'

She hesitated. 'Yes, of course.' It was the best response she could muster, and it constrained her doubts.

Birds perched on the edge of the river were fighting over crumbs of food left behind, and the worn-out old bench beneath them shook in the wind. The sky looked hazy and the rooftops in the distance gave her a sense of home. Memories of her childhood were here on the river, in this city.

Miloš turned to face her and watched her playing with the tassles on the end of her scarf.

'Marry me, Jana. Marry me!'

There was a stunned silence and she looked at him head-on. She saw an eager expectancy in his eyes, a desperation for a response from a girl who he hadn't seen for so long.

'Miloš, I...I don't know what to say. I can't answer you now. I need time. When? When did you plan this? What about your studies?'

'Just give me an answer. Stop asking questions and tell me what you want. You must know, deep down. You know who I am. Do you want to be with me? Is it a yes or a no, Jana?'

Here was a boy holding out a present that she wasn't sure whether to accept or refuse. His face dropped. All the recent

221

events with Lukas flashed through her mind. But she also remembered the times she shared with Miloš – the night when she wore the red dress, fighting in the snow, meeting him at the train station in Prague. He had felt familiar and exciting at the same time.

Despite the distance over the months, he hadn't changed as much as she had. He was still the same boy she had fallen in love with, and he hadn't played games with her or led her on. Better still, he hadn't deceived her.

Jana hugged him. She couldn't let go, partly out of a fear of having to give a clearer answer, but partly because she was reminded of the scent of his skin – fresh, comforting. His hair ran coarsely through her fingers. She pulled away and fiddled with the button of her shirt.

'Miloš, I love you. I know that much. I haven't been very good at keeping in contact and writing or phoning, but I've missed you. Life has been complicated since you left.' She looked out towards the water, the light caught the ripples as boats passed. 'I need to think. I won't make you wait forever, Miloš. We haven't seen each other for all this time, and I've changed.'

'We'll carry on seeing each other,' he said. 'Is that all right?'

The sun had vanished, but the deep colours of the evening light were beautiful. She looked at him slowly, purposefully. Maybe she was still the same girl who had jumped on a train to Letovice, the same girl who listened to Tatínek and his thoughts and opinions. She missed him so much, but only when she allowed herself to think of him. She missed his wisdom. How would he feel if he knew about Miloš' proposal? She knew he would have liked Miloš, realising the regret in the fact that they had never met. They were like-minded in their approach to life – talkers, doers, kind-hearted men, both of them. Jana cupped one side of his face in her hand and looked at him for a while.

'Miloš, let's just take time, enjoy the minutes that pass. Let's not rush. I need to sort things out in my mind. When I'm ready I'll tell you everything. I just want us to have fun, see places together. But know that I love you.'

It wasn't a phrase she used lightly, and it wasn't one she used often. He nodded, jumped up and took her hand.

'Shall we?' He held his arm out with a wry smile. 'Let's walk.' It reminded her of their dance in the Martineks' front room.

He led her along the river and back to the familiar city streets with a look that said he had already won her.

'I had a lovely evening, Miloš. I'm glad you're back. I've wondered what this would feel like, and it's good. Thank you for asking me, I appreciate your patience, and I know you want the best. That means a great deal to me.'

'Jana you are very special. The distance didn't change anything, it just made this moment later than I had hoped. I knew, when I dropped you off at the train station in Letovice, I knew then that I wanted to be with you. It was just a matter of waiting for our lives to run their course – and the small issue of geography – before I could ask you.'

'Geography shouldn't have stopped you from asking. You could have put it in writing.'

'That's a thought,' he smiled. 'I wanted to ask you face to face and brave your reaction.'

'Miloš, the name I used by mistake the other day...

'What about it?' He turned towards her with a look of concern. They had reached the door of his apartment and were standing at the entrance holding hands. He was close to her, their feet almost touching.

'Miloš, I was seeing him while you were gone.'

'I did wonder, but I couldn't bring myself to ask. To be honest, I didn't really want to know.'

'I'm sorry. I should have waited, I was just searching, searching for something or someone to keep me anchored. Everything has changed so much and there's very little to hang on to at the moment.'

'I understand. I didn't expect you to just wait. I just hoped that you might.'

'He betrayed my father.'

'How?'

Jana couldn't face retelling the scenario but she needed to tell him in her own words.

'They were in prison at the same time. He wrote a letter, which kept Tatínek in prison for longer than he should have been inside.'

There was more of a look of understanding in his face, than shock. 'Jana, I'm so sorry.'

'He betrayed Tatínek with a lie, an incrimination.' Her

words ran away, free from constraint. 'He might have survived if he hadn't been incarcerated for so long. His lungs were bad. They all suffered but those who stayed the longest rarely survived into old age. That lie stole the father I should have had, it stole from our family.' She started to break down.

Miloš pulled her towards him and waited, waited until her words ceased. 'Will you come in, just for a while?'

'Yes,' she said, needing his presence.

Surprisingly, she had slept well, having crept in through the front door at some point in the early hours of the morning. Jana wanted to see Lukas. She needed to clarify things in her mind, having just seen Miloš. After breakfast she picked up the post, as usual, and went to her room to freshen up. She didn't want to turn up looking like a young barn owl, which is what her hair would have threatened to turn her into if it hadn't seen a brush in the mornings.

Hearing her sister arrive, she ran to the front door.

'Irena. How are you?'

'Jana, I just came over to give Matka some cake tins I borrowed.' She handed them to Matka with a small bunch of wild flowers. Everything OK, Jana? You look preoccupied with something.' Her sister knew her well. 'Come on, tell me. I know when you're up to something.'

Jana didn't know whether to tell Matka or her sister about the proposal, or respond to her sister's question. Irena always wanted answers. Jana didn't have Irena's clear-cut mind and her feelings dominated almost all of her decisions, so it was difficult to share anything which didn't already have an answer. Sometimes, conversations without answers felt like interrogations.

'That Miloš boy is back in town,' added Matka.

'Oh?' said Irena, almost as though she was asking a question. 'Have you seen him yet, Jana?'

'Last night, yes,' she responded quietly, hoping her sister wouldn't hear.

They both looked at her and waited for more information.

'Well, how did it go? What did he say?'

Jana wondered why her family asked so many questions. It felt like an invasion of her privacy. They were just interested, and she knew they were curious.

'Good, good. We just talked, you know. Nothing special.'

How could she say that, with the proposal in her mind?

'He's well, busy with university, medicine.'

'And what did you talk about?'

She should have known better than to imagine she could ward off more questions. They hadn't seen each other for a while, and Irena knew how much Jana liked Miloš. They had talked in the evenings, on long walks through the city about love and life, and her sister knew her well.

'Let's meet up this week,' said Irena, 'and we'll catch up properly.'

'OK. See you soon.' Jana leaned in to kiss Irena on the cheek and left, closing the front door behind her, leaving Irena with Matka.

'She's a flighty thing at the moment,' said Matka. 'Can't

pin her down. She seems worried about – I don't know – something.' She picked up the bag Irena had brought and turned to unload the implements into various drawers, drawers which had the same old wooden spoons and cake tins as when they were younger.

'Thank you for the flowers,' said Matka, arranging them in a vase. She breathed in the scent of the wild blossom.

'Is everything OK?' said Irena. 'Has something happened?'

'I don't know, Miloš rang the other day and she seemed jumpy, even before she saw him yesterday evening, but this morning there's clearly something more on her mind.'

Irena started to dry the mugs by the sink. She put the kettle on as if she was still living there, and pulled two ceramic mugs down from the shelf. Matka rarely said no to a coffee, and Irena was too intrigued about Jana to take the time to ask if she wanted one. She didn't want to derail the conversation. Not now.

'I saw Lukas yesterday and he seems distracted as well.' She tried to elicit a response from Matka.

'I know what you mean,' said Matka. 'I don't know what's going on but Jana seems more, I don't know, closed-off. She's been somewhere else in her mind. I'm sure there's something bothering her, but I can't get her to talk. You know what she's like when she's worried.'

'Serious? Quiet?' said Irena.

'Yes, it concerns me when she won't talk, but I'm sure she'll work things out in her own time. We just have to wait. You girls certainly are different. I often wonder how the three

227

of you can be from the same mould. I used to look at you each as children, and wonder how you would grow and change.'

Matka held her daughter's face, leaning over the damp drying-up towel and a warm coffee, and smiled as she looked into her eyes.

'You know, you were the one I used to worry about because you were so particular about everything, so precise. I thought life wouldn't live up to your expectations. But now… now I worry about Jana. She seems disappointed, let down by life, and she doesn't seem to be able to get over the loss of Tatínek.'

'We all miss him, Matka.'

'I know, my sweet girl, but I wonder whether she just hasn't yet let go. She seems to be doing everything in her power to keep everything the same. I can't put my finger on what is troubling her, but there's something. She used to be so full of fun. Remember?'

'Yes, but things change, Matka, people change, and you never completely know someone else's heart or mind.'

Irena put the coffee mug down. She turned and looked out of the kitchen window at the birds, which had just landed on the tree.

'They're so carefree, aren't they?'

'I just want you all to be happy, that's all a mother wants for her children. I don't want to see any of you weighed down by things, by situations, trials.'

Irena hugged Matka. Her head barely reached the neckline of Irena's top.

'She'll be fine, Matka, you'll see. Don't you worry, we're all OK. Jana's a fighter, she'll come through, whatever it is.'

Matka nodded and moved over to the table to go through the post. As Irena watched her, she saw a woman who had adjusted to being on her own. A woman who was content with life as she now knew it. It never felt the same now, coming to the house without Tatínek working in his study or sitting with a paper.

Chapter 26

Lukas opened the door slowly holding the phone to his ear. His shirt was half buttoned-up, possibly not in the right holes. He was barefoot and crumpled. He looked good that way. Jana liked the way he didn't try to create any particular impression. He was the same first thing in the morning and the afternoon – with the exception of protective clothing – and hadn't changed by the evening if he went out.

His socks were hanging out of his trouser pocket, waiting to reach his feet. He must have pulled them out of a drawer and been distracted, maybe by the phone ringing.

'Jana, give me a minute,' he said, trying to get rid of whoever was on the phone. 'Help yourself to a coffee.'

And with that he disappeared into the bedroom. She could hear mumbling and muffled laughter as he closed the door behind him. She felt nervous, nervous about so many things.

They hadn't cleared the air from their tense meeting and her anger was still raw. The proposal from Miloš had confused her and she hoped that seeing Lukas would help to provide the answer.

The lady opposite was hanging towels out of the windows to dry. The tiled rooftops replicated a pattern which went on for miles, like cracked pavements. The reds and greys had become faded and broken with time, and the layers were now out of place like a random puzzle. She imagined how they must have looked when they were newer, fresher, but now they were worn and tired. It gave them character, a story, and a life.

The way things changed and weathered with time was different in each circumstance but the rooftops were comforting to her, a reminder of times past, offering a familiarity that she now craved. She had been missing Tatínek in recent weeks, and the memories of her childhood had started to fade. Jana didn't want to let go or to forget. Even the times with the Martinek family in Letovice had become hazy. The revelations of her father's time in prison made her cling to what she knew. So much had changed – been taken away – that she wondered if the political changes were going to gather momentum and make the country unrecognisable. She didn't want anything to change, except perhaps the confusion over Miloš and Lukas.

'Jana, I'm sorry for the delay.' He rarely apologised, but he looked ruffled. She wondered who he'd been talking to but didn't want to ask. She didn't feel it was her business – it would be wrong to look too intrigued.

Fighting back memories of the night they spent together was proving difficult. Standing now in the living room looking at a man who she loved – despite his betrayal –was more complicated than she had anticipated. Jana was losing her grip on what she wanted.

Lukas reached into his pocket and pulled out a notebook – a worn-looking brown notebook with creased corners. It looked as though it had taken up residence in his pocket some time ago.

'Here,' he said, 'I've been wanting to share this with you ever since you found the first one.' He looked uncomfortable.

'The first one?' She wasn't sure if she could face any more facts or any more truths. She wanted it all to stop, to vanish without a trace.

'Read it,' he insisted, placing it into the palm of her hand, as though he was handing her something fragile.

'I don't know if I can, Lukas. I'm not sure.'

'Please.' I need you to know before…'

'Before what?'

'Just read it, please.'

He sat down on the brown sofa in a spot that had clearly just been occupied. She opened the small notebook and leafed through the pages, then went back to the beginning and started to read slowly, carefully, so as not to miss anything. Moving the cushions out of the way, she leant back and frowned.

'I don't know how you'll feel but I need you to know, Jana. I need you to know the whole truth.'

She looked up at him briefly then carried on reading,

absorbing each word and turning each page with fear and dread. What more could there be to know?

Detailed accounts of their every move had been logged with frightening precision – her father's contacts and phone calls, his meetings with ministers, her mother's phone calls. Every item of post that had been intercepted had been recorded. Their lives were here in print for the secret service to trawl through, to judge, and to punish. How could her father's loss of life ever be atoned for?

'Lukas, how is this supposed to help me? Is it meant to make you feel better…that I know? I can't read any more.' She threw the book down on to the floor and stood up. 'I've had enough of this and I don't want to hear any more. Do you understand me?'

'I do, I just wanted you to know before I asked you to marry me.'

'Marry you? Is this a trick question?'

Seemingly undaunted, he continued. 'I would have asked you sooner if I hadn't been hiding all of this. I just can't go any further with you when there is more to know.'

Two proposals in the space of two days, this was like a muddled dream. One from someone she hadn't seen for months, and the other from someone who had snatched the life away from her family.

She loved them both, but in different ways and would find it difficult to let either of them go, but marriage? She hadn't thought that far ahead and wasn't the sort of girl who had spent her life wishing for a husband or children. There was too much else to do. She wanted to work, and to change people's lives. There was so much that she wanted to achieve, maybe start a physiotherapy centre of her own, set up a charity, become a journalist, or study politics. She hadn't factored marriage to the mix. In reality Jana thought she might be better alone.

'So, do you have an answer?' He stood with his hands in his pockets, reminding her of a young boy.

'Lukas, I can't say yes but it's not a no.'

'I want you to know that I want to be with you,' he said.

Lukas got down on one knee. He looked disappointed and hopeful at the same time. Maybe the expression on her face didn't help matters. The way he was behaving was endearing. She felt a sense of his guilt and pain, and knew that she hadn't seen the situation from his point of view. So much time had been spent licking her wounds that she hadn't given his a second thought.

'Lukas, wait. I need to say something. I just want to tell you that I'm sorry for not understanding, for not seeing into your world, for not understanding what you went through, and for not forgiving you. I do, I really do.'

He grasped her hands. 'Marry me.'

'Lukas, I don't know what to say.'

She felt a surge of love for him, compassion even, in the face of the adversity that he had endured. Knowing she would never understand the depths of his despair in prison, his darkest hours, spurred her on to forgiveness. She wanted to wash the past away and to move forward. It was difficult to know how.

'I want to give you the answer you're looking for, but I'm going to ask you to wait.'

She wanted so much to say 'yes', but it didn't feel right with the proposal from Miloš left open. She couldn't face telling Lukas about yesterday, and her head was aching from the tension.

'I understand, Jana. I'll wait.'

He got up and held her for a while. 'I know you need time, but I also know how I feel about you. When I look to the future I always hope it will involve you.'

She grasped him tightly. His bookshelf was in her line of vision. She wished she could say yes, but something stopped her. Her gaze fell on the photograph of his mother and she wondered about this small frame of a lady. What would she have said if she had known what her son had done to a whole family, to many families? Would she have understood? Would she have forgiven him and stuck by him, given all that she, too, had endured? She was a mother, of course she would, any parent would.

'Lukas, I can only imagine the trauma of having to hide all of this.' She nodded in the direction of the bookshelves where the notebooks had fallen on the floor. 'I want to bury it now, move on. We need some sort of closure. It's tormented us both for too long. The country is moving on, but I've tried not to. I've resisted everything. I've resisted change. I couldn't let anything change in case I lost anything else that was precious to me.'

'I understand, Jana. I need to go, but I'll call you.'

She nodded, and he kissed her on the cheek, lingering close enough that she could feel his breath.

She left with mixed feelings. Lukas no longer had anything to hide but it would be difficult to ever really trust him. Although having two proposals was confusing, it was also flattering that both men wanted to be with her. In her heart she loved them both.

Lukas was captivating on so many levels, but Miloš was a steady constant in her mind with a strength that she felt she didn't have inside herself at the moment. Shouldn't that be what she wanted?

Chapter 27

The clouds were closing in and he wanted to make it on time. Getting into his Skoda, Lukas remembered that he had left his wallet in the kitchen. He usually remembered to slip it into his back pocket, but he was in a rush. He got out of the car, crossed the street and put his key in the lock. After a quick scan of the surfaces in his apartment he found it resting on the kitchen window ledge, where it had been left the night before. At least it had accompanied him back from the bar. The car took a while to start. A friend who had moved away – and had no need for it any more – had given it to him. A generous gift, Lukas had thought at the time.

The journey out of Prague was slow. Heading east from the city, he passed the familiar sights and wondered how much they would change with time. Jana had made him start to question everything. It should be under an hour if he travelled smoothly out towards Melnik. He'd managed it in forty minutes on one journey, but it wasn't guaranteed. A pretty part of Bohemia, it lay on the Labe and Vltava rivers just north of Prague. It was rural, agricultural land and boasted a beautiful Renaissance-style castle with, as he remembered, large wine cellars. Having been seized by the Communist Party under their rule, it had now been returned to the princes of Lobcowicz.

Lukas liked to visit the unmarked Jewish cemetery in the town. He would read the inscriptions on the gravestones and try to imagine who these people were, the individuals who no longer existed on this earth, the stories they might have told, and the history they might have shared. Many of the weathered inscriptions were in Hebrew, Czech and German. Lukas could read all three languages, although his Hebrew was not as sharp as his German and Czech. He had learned the latter two languages at school and, growing up, he had used Czech with his friends, but his mother spoke to him in Hebrew.

Lukas had felt drawn to his Jewish roots from an early age, and visiting the cemetery in the town where members of his family were buried felt cathartic. It was a way of remembering, a way of feeling closer to his mother. Although this time he wondered if it would remind him of meeting Jana at the cemetery in Josefov. She was the only person who had ever seen him crying.

He couldn't get her out of his mind. He had hoped to spend more time with her before he left, but his work had been busy with the castle restorations in full swing. The months had gathered momentum as they passed.

Taking the second left on to Revolucni, he wondered what her answer would be. Had she really forgiven him, or were there still doubts in her mind? It was difficult to imagine a future with or without her. It didn't really matter now.

He needed some form of redemption, and marriage couldn't provide that for him. The memories of the past haunted him, despite her professed absolution. He hadn't truly forgiven himself, and that was the crux of it all. He couldn't get over the utter destruction inflicted on the lives that he had touched.

There were days when he wanted to vanish, remove his stain from the landscape, but he fought through the despair. His work was lonely, and he had too many hours to think and deliberate. When he replaced tiny pieces of each section of the mosaic, the concentration that was needed became intense, but there was a part of his mind that was left unchecked and free to wander. This was where he had been taken into dark places. The nightmares replayed over and over. The system had been torn down, but it had left its poison. The memories were too powerful to overcome. Some days were bearable, but others dragged him through the accusations and the humiliation. How had he been turned? How could he have lived a different life?

But he hadn't, and the past was now permanently etched with his mistakes. This was his life, one in which he struggled to continue. Jana had forgiven him but he hadn't forgiven himself. He was still in a prison waiting for freedom, waiting for a day of escape. There had to be a way out, a way of leaving the lives of those around him intact.

The note sat on the passenger seat, waiting to be read. He had taken it out of his wallet and placed it there earlier, before pulling out of his street. As the car neared the bend in the road he turned the steering wheel hard right and slammed his food on the accelerator. The car spun out of control and the edge of the road rotated around the windows until he could see the tree nearing the driver door. Flashes of sunlight blinded his vision.

He closed his eyes.

Jana heard a knock at the door. It was a girl, probably a few years older. She looked eerily like Lukas and had the same piercing eyes and curly dark hair.

'You must be Jana.'

'Do I know you?'

The girl looked pained or in a state of shock. 'I'm Lukas's sister, Monika. Can I...can I come in?'

Jana opened the door wider, took her coat, and led her into the kitchen, wondering why she had been paid this unexpected visit.

'Coffee?' She saw the hesitation on the girl's face. 'I've already made some.'

'Thank you.' Monika sat down carefully.

'I have some bad news, I'm sorry.'

Jana's heart sank. She had never met Lukas's sister and wasn't even aware of her existence, until now. Lukas always kept his cards close to his chest, and maybe the turmoil of his past had eclipsed the need to speak about family.

'There's been an accident, a bad accident.'

Jana lowered her head, feeling her blood pulsing through her body. She knew this could only involve Lukas. He was all they had in common.

'Lukas was on his way to visit me and his car...'

'What happened?' Jana reached over to grasp Monika's arm. Monika stumbled over the words, grasping her mug of coffee, as if it would save her from falling.

'His car went off the road and hit a tree.'

'Is he all right? How bad is it?'

'Jana, he didn't make it. He didn't survive the impact. The car is a mess.'

Her last few words were followed by a long silence. Neither of them knew what to say. Jana felt sick. The proposal, and their conversations, flooded into her mind.

Monika looked up. 'The police don't know if it was an accident.'

'What do you mean?' The words were detached from her lips.

'They're treating it as a possible suicide.'

'No. Why? Why would he...'

Monika looked at Jana head-on. 'He had written a note. The police found it crumpled on the floor. He'd just left the cemetery in my town and had nearly reached the house.'

Jana gasped and clasped both hands around her mouth, as if to stifle any exclamation. The physical pain in her chest gripped her tightly.

'Jana, are you OK? You look pale. What can I do?'

Monika found a glass on the side and filled it with cold water. As she turned around with the glass in her hand, Jana collapsed on the floor on to her knees. She curled her head into her torso, holding her body in a foetal position, and sobbed.

Monika knelt down beside her.

'Jana, I know he proposed. He was on the phone to me when you arrived, and he had told me he was going to ask you. He was on his way to see me when we lost him.'

The word 'we' repeated itself in her mind. There were many people who were going to be affected by this.

'He didn't talk about you,' said Jana. 'I didn't know he had a sister.'

'He was a very private person. He learned to keep things to himself, and his time in prison almost shut him down completely. His emotions were tightly packed away from that point in his life. He was so excited about the proposal, about you. Jana, he was in love with you.'

Jana nodded slowly and listened in disbelief. Monika continued to talk. She heard none of the words.

'He talked about you all the time and he wanted us to meet. I just never imagined it would be like this. The police called me and I knew I had to come and see you. I wanted to tell you in person. I wanted to meet you.'

'You've lost your brother. I shouldn't be reacting like this. Monika, I'm sorry for your loss and that I didn't get to meet you with him.'

'I know and thank you. You don't have to explain.' Jana hugged her, but Monika pulled away abruptly.

'The funeral will be next week, just outside Melnik, if you want to be there.'

'Melnik?' said Jana.

'Yes, it's where we're from. Didn't he tell you?'

'No.' Jana's voice dropped. 'He didn't, he said he was from Prague. I didn't know that he hadn't grown up in the city.'

'It's where I live, where he was heading to when...when it happened.'

Her sentence ground to a halt. She must have realised how little Jana knew about him. Why hadn't Lukas told her where he was from, told her about the existence of his sister? He'd left many unanswered questions. He would never have a chance to hear her answer to his question.

Jana watched Monika as she continued to speak. The way her mouth moved, the way her curls fell into the nape of her neck, her hand gestures. It was as though Lukas was with them, in the room. Observing his features and so many of his mannerisms, in the form of his sister, felt strange. Monika had a fire in her eyes and a look of determination. She was steely and collected for someone who was sharing the news of a death.

Chapter 28

The church filled with people. She hadn't set foot in a church building since Irena's wedding. They should have been in a synagogue, it would have been more appropriate, but his sister insisted that the funeral be held in their home town. It was understandable. Jana hoped that he had found peace before he died. She believed in a higher power but she didn't subscribe to the idea that people needed forgiveness from anyone other than another human being.

Many milestones were remembered within the walls of these buildings – births, deaths, marriages – all documented in the record books. Lives had been celebrated through baptisms, matrimony or funerals. It seemed a harsh reality to be remembering a life cut short, ended so abruptly, and without a confirmed reason. The funeral was a sombre occasion rather than a celebration. The unanswered question of 'how' loomed over the day like a storm cloud. The hymn played slowly as she thought through what might have pushed him to suicide, if that was the truth. She could deal with the pain more clearly if it had been an accident, but suicide? Was she implicated in this? Had memories of prison haunted him beyond what he could bear? Had he still struggled with memories of her father?

Her hands were shaking, and her chest felt squeezed by a constricting pain. She waited until the last hymn and slipped out quietly. It would be difficult to know what to say to anyone, and she had already spoken to Lukas's sister before the service. The rest of his life seemed a mystery, and she wasn't officially engaged before he had died so she didn't want to greet people and have to explain, neither did she feel it was right to be grieving in public. The burial was just for close friends and relatives. She nodded to Irena and Benes, and left through the side door. There was a small opening to the graveyard where numerous tombstones stood imposingly on the grass and pebbles.

The sky looked bleak with dark rolling clouds overhead, and it was starting to rain. She had difficulty seeing the gates at the end of the pathway and, in her state of shock, Jana had forgotten her umbrella. She ran through the rain to the train station as the drops ricocheted off the pavements. She could hear thunder in the distance.

The journey back to Prague was a blur. She was tired and deeply sad. Irena and Benes had offered her a lift back after the funeral, but she wanted to go home alone. Monika had invited them, but she couldn't face it. Jana needed to be alone to grieve silently. Grief always needed its own silence and isolation.

To Jana's surprise, as the train drew in to the station, she could see Miloš waiting for her on the platform. His face was a welcome reminder of home. As she stumbled out of the carriage he held her close.

'How did you know I'd be here?' she asked, wondering if he knew about Lukas.

'I couldn't get hold of you, so I went to your apartment. Your mother told me about the accident. I'm so sorry for your loss, Jana. I had no idea.' She buried her head into his jacket.

'Did he really propose? Two proposals?'

'Miloš, I'm sorry for not telling you about him. You were away, and then when you came back I didn't know how to explain. His proposal, and your proposal, they both took me by surprise. I'm still reeling. I didn't know what to say.'

She regretted telling Matka about Lukas's proposal. Miloš deserved to hear the news first hand. It didn't matter now. He was gone. She couldn't grasp the idea that she would never see him again, never give him an answer. It was so final, a door had closed that no one could reopen.

Seeing Miloš was comforting, but she longed to talk to Lukas just one last time, to see his face and to hear his voice, to tell him that she still loved him, and that it was all over. The past had gone and they could start afresh.

He was gone.

He would never know if she would spend the rest of her life with him. She would never have answers to the many questions that still raced through her mind in the dark hours of the night.

'Are you OK, Jana?' Miloš walked alongside her towards the exit of the station, with one arm across her shoulder.

She hesitated, 'Yes, I'm OK. Thank you for coming to get me.'

'I thought you might need some company.'

She climbed into his car, and appreciated his kindness and sensitivity.

'Your mother has been worried about you. She told me about the proposal so that you didn't have to. Do you want me to take you home?'

'No, can I come to you for a while?'

Miloš had a student apartment that she had been to several times, and she needed to be away from her home just for a few hours. They pulled into his road. It was dimly lit in the early evening light, and she could see the city lights beyond the row of apartment blocks. She'd missed the uncomplicated comfort of knowing who he was and how he felt about her.

As they walked into his kitchen and turned on the light she pulled him towards her and kissed him. He took a step back and stroked her hair.

'Jana, I can give you space if that's what you need. I know this must be a really difficult time for you, and you don't need any more complications.'

Refusing to answer, she kissed him again, then shook her

head. 'No, Miloš, I'm fine.'

She hadn't used his name for a while. Jana ran her arms down to his hands and clasped them tightly. She led him to his room without saying anything and he walked behind her, smiling an invisible smile. They passed posters on the walls of bands that he liked and odd bits of washing hanging up. His place made her feel safe. It was familiar to her only because the belongings were his.

They sat on the small sofa in his room. It was, typically, without any cushions. She lifted her legs up and held her knees, relaxing back into the corner of the sofa. She leaned on one arm which threatened to give way at any moment.

The light pushing through the net curtains was dim and she scanned the shelves for any new photos. He liked pictures of people – friends, family and old black and white photographs of familiar places.

She saw a picture of her smiling with Kamila from their days in Letovice. She had changed. He had changed. They were different people now and she still loved him. She loved his gentleness, his understated approach, and his ability to just listen to her thoughts.

He was so different from Lukas in a way that she never cared to admit, and now she felt she couldn't compare them. It was disrespectful and irrelevant. The deep ache from losing him hadn't and wouldn't subside, but the pain clarified her thoughts.

'Miloš, I want to marry you. I want to be with you. Yes, is my answer. It's long overdue and I know I've made you wait, but...'

'Yes?' He hesitated before sitting up. 'Is that a yes? Are you sure you want to make that decision so soon? You've only just lost him.'

She put a finger on his lips and nodded slowly.

'I do. It's OK. I've been thinking about it all for a while, about you and about him.' She wasn't prepared to ignore the previous existence of Lukas just because he had gone, because he had died so cruelly.

'Miloš, I loved him, I have to admit that, but I loved you too and I still do. Of course, I enjoyed the excitement of you both, but I want to be with you.'

She didn't like to talk about either of them in the past tense, but couldn't find any other way of expressing her thoughts.

'But don't you want to take time to think, to really consider...to grieve?'

Maybe he felt guilty for having pushed her initially, or regretted letting her go when he left for the Philippines.

'No, I don't need more time. I want to move on.' She hesitated. 'With you, Miloš, with you.'

She held his gaze as she said the last two words, to see what his eyes were telling her. He stood up and embraced her with one hand on the back of her head. She remembered the way he kissed her. Life, her life at least, had been a series of losses, but what was given in return far outweighed them.

'There is something I need to tell you,' she said.

'Go on.' His eyes widened.

'Miloš, I'm pregnant!'

'Is it...?'

'Yes, the baby is yours.'

She saw his hesitation. 'I only had that kind of a relationship with Lukas once, a long time ago, which is why I know it's yours.' It felt strange to talk about her past with Lukas. 'Looking back I should have known that I wanted to be with you, but it was confusing.'

He looked relieved as he rearranged his sweater.

'At the time I thought that we shouldn't have,' she said, 'not so soon, but I know now that it was meant to be. I know I've been a bit distant, and I'm sorry. Please give me a chance, give all three of us a chance.' She put her hand on her stomach.

'Jana, stop,' he said. 'I asked you to marry me. I've thought about it for a long time and I'm not about to change my mind. You don't have to feel scared. We're OK.' He rubbed her tummy gently and smiled.

His smile gave her peace. He knew how to make her feel calmer.

'We have to tell Matka. I have to see her.'

'I asked her if I could marry you.'

'You did?'

'Yes, in the absence of your father, I thought it was the right thing to do.'

'That's really thoughtful,' said Jana. 'She would have liked that, he would have liked that. Tatínek, I mean.' Miloš nodded. Kindness – his kindness – erased so much of the pain. It was a rare attribute to find in people, at least in her experience.

'You were waiting until I'd figured things out?' said Jana.

'Something like that, but you've had so much to deal with. I knew you'd need time.'

'Time is too short for some and too long for others. You never know how long you'll…'

'It's OK, Jana. We don't have to talk about it. I just want you to be happy. I want us to be happy. I know you miss him and I know how much you miss your father. I can't replace either of them, but I want to be enough for you.'

'I only need to know that you're there. That's enough, Miloš. Who you are is enough.'

He glanced at the photographs. 'We have a new life to think about now.'

She walked home the following morning to find Matka sitting at the table kitchen.

'Jana, I have something for you.' Matka handed her an envelope and Jana sat down opposite. 'It's from your father. I kept it for so long. I didn't know when to give it to you but he wrote it just before…when his health deteriorated he asked me to keep it until you were ready.'

'Do you know what it says?' Jana asked.

Matka nodded. 'I didn't know when would be a good time.'

Jana slid her finger along the top edge of the white envelope and peeled it back slowly. She pulled out the letter and unfolded it. Tatínek's writing was so familiar. His black ink pen had scrawled words across the page in a sea of swirls and dashes. She had trouble reading his writing when she was younger. Jana held the paper to her nose and breathed in deeply. There was no scent of him, just his words.

My dear Jana,

I met a man in prison. His name was Lukas, and he taught me that life is long and life is short. He taught me that people want to do good, in whatever form they believe that to be. We will all do things that we regret and will have to live with the consequences. He told me that the regime would be over one day and that we would move on and meet new people, hold our families in our arms and find a new purpose, a new cause to fight. I know whole-heartedly that if you believe in something enough you should fight for it, whatever it might cost you. For the pain that I caused you and your brother and sister in being away, I am sorry. I would do it all again for the freedom that it will bring your children, and for their children's children. I know there are battles that rage in your mind, and my hope is that you find peace and joy in your life. You need to love without being afraid, and hope without doubting. Find peace in the storm, my girl, and all will be well. I see so much of myself in you.

My point is that my friend, Lukas, he saved me. He saved me from the agonizing days spent inside, and he also saved me on a day when I wanted to bring an end to my own life. You see, he knew there would be better days ahead, and he had strength. He took away the items I was going to use because he knew. He knew about you all, and about Matka. He knew I would escape, and that you needed me to come home. My hope is that you find somebody like him, someone who will fight for you, someone who teaches you to keep going when you can't go on. Believe in yourself, Jana, and believe also in others. Trust them.

Václav Havel said this:

'Hope is a state of mind, not of the world. Hope, in this deep and powerful sense, is not the same as joy that things are going well, or willingness to invest in enterprises that are obviously heading for success, but rather an ability to work for something because it is good.'

My sweet girl, if you can glean anything from these wise words, and from the fact that my friend saved me in so many ways, have hope. Hope is a powerful force in any circumstance in your life. Without it there is little purpose in what you do. Know that the world is both good and bad, it is both changing and static. There are so many paradoxes, but there are many that you can shape. Live your life and live it to the full, knowing that your days are numbered and purposed.

All my love and kisses,
Tatínek

Acknowledgements

I would like to thank those who have encouraged me along the journey of writing my first novel. To Dr Charles W.R.D. Moseley, whose invaluable teaching inspired my love of English literature and of the written word. To Saša and Michael Šafránek, without whom my immersion into Czech life and culture at a unique turning point in history might not have occurred. At a time in which the political changes had resulted in the split of Czechoslovakia and the emergence of the new Czech and Slovak Republics, I thank you for your insights and your friendship. The experience of Prague and Letovice, while it remained relatively untouched by tourism, has left an indelible imprint in my memory. My acknowledgements go to the Getty Conservation Institute for the published papers from an international symposium marking the completion of a ten-year project to conserve the Last Judgement mosaic at St. Vitus Cathedral, Prague. The unique photographs and papers gave me a glimpse into the life of the character of Lukas. To my editors Rob and Lucy for their skilled work in reviewing the manuscript, thank you for your wise advice and keen eye for detail.

If you would like to be kept up to date with F.C. Malby's author news please go to http://www.fcmalby.com and sign up to the mailing list. You can also connect with the author via the social media sites listed on the website.